TALES OF THE UNDERGROUND RAILROAD

BRIGHT  FREEDOM'S SONG

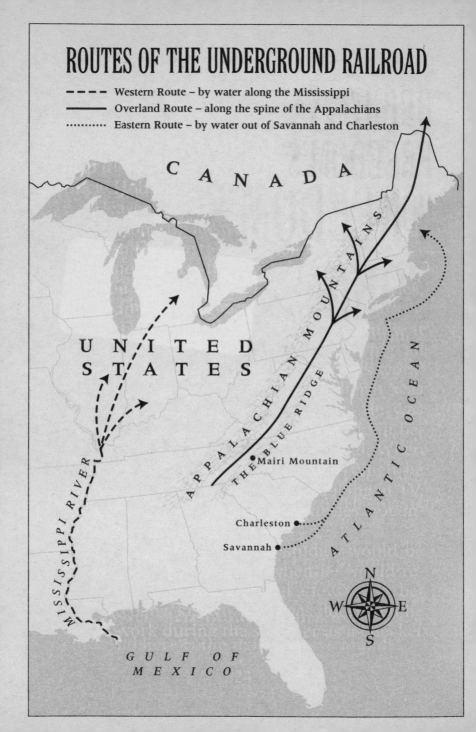

BRIGHT ❧

FREEDOM'S

SONG *A Story of the Underground Railroad*

GLORIA HOUSTON

SCHOLASTIC INC.
New York Toronto London Auckland Sydney
Mexico City New Delhi Hong Kong

ISBN 0-439-13849-3

Published by Scholastic Inc., 555 Broadway, New York, NY 10012,
by arrangement with Harcourt Brace & Company.
SCHOLASTIC and associated logos are trademarks and/or registered
trademarks of Scholastic Inc.

12 11 10 9 8 7 6 5 4 3 2 1   9/9 0 1 2 3 4/0

Printed in the U.S.A.   40

First Scholastic printing, October 1999

Text set in Meridien
Designed by Linda Lockowitz

To Diane, my daughter,
who gave her personality to Marcus

In 1876 abolitionist Levi Coffin wrote that the success of the Underground Railroad in aiding escaping slaves was largely due to the work of slaves, former slaves, and the yeoman farmers of the South. I credit his work as the inspiration for this book.

PREFACE ᴥ

When I was a child, I heard stories of past events in the southern Appalachian Mountains from older residents of my community. I was fascinated that many times those stories and the "facts" I read in my history texts did not present the same information.

Locations of hiding places for escaping slaves before and during the Civil War were a part of such stories, but my texts discussed only the work of the Underground Railroad in Ohio and New England, far north of the states where slavery was legal. Slaves had to walk many miles through the South with no maps, food, or supplies before they reached the free states. The overland route north, traveled by more than 50,000 slaves, ran along the Greater Appalachian Mountain chain (Breyfogle, 1958).

With the hindsight provided by the passing of more than 125 years, we may think that opposing slavery and aiding escaping slaves was the only possible moral and ethical choice. However, to those who lived in states where slavery was considered both a legal and a moral practice, to take a stand against slavery took extreme commitment to the belief that slavery was a moral wrong.

Levi Coffin was a leading abolitionist in Ohio. He wrote in 1868 that although abolitionists wrote about the Underground Railroad, he believed that far more of the work of the Railroad was done by slaves who would not or could not escape, by former slaves who had escaped, and by the yeoman farmers of the South—those owners of small farms who usually did not own slaves.

As a child sitting across the river from a cave generally acknowledged to be a stop on the Underground Railroad, I listened as "Uncle Robert" Wiseman, the oldest man in my community, told stories of his great-grandfather's escape from the bondage of indentureship in the 1760s. He told of the long walk from Charleston, South Carolina, to the valley where his great-grandfather, young William Wiseman, homesteaded the land on which we sat. William Wiseman was the first of my ancestors to arrive in America.

I have always assumed a connection between anti-slavery activities in the region and the previous indentureships of many of the earliest settlers. During the extensive research I conducted while writing this novel, I did not find documentation of such a connection by historical researchers, but what I did find has convinced me that the connection is a valid one.

I am astounded by the similarities between the experiences of indentured Europeans and those of African slaves. In fact, one historian wrote that the British slave traders did nothing to Africans they had not already practiced on their neighbors. For many years, the truth of the horrors experienced by African Americans and

American-born slaves was ignored. In most recent years, a more accurate picture of those experiences has emerged. However, the experiences of Europeans in American bondage continue to be ignored by writers of history texts and fiction.

Many of the earliest settlers of the Appalachian Mountains walked there following their release from indentureship. Two generations later, the Wiseman farm hid a cave, a cave that was a stop on the Underground Railroad. I believe there is a connection between the location of a safe place for escaping slaves on the Wiseman farm and the experiences of William Wiseman as an indentured servant in bondage.

To connect these two parallel and important parts of our history, I felt this book needed to be written.

BRIGHT FREEDOM'S SONG

PROLOGUE ∂◯
1862

WITH TREMBLING HANDS, Bright held the reins, keeping her eyes focused straight ahead as six horsemen rode single file past the wagon. With all the courage she could find in her fifteen-year-old self, she silently drew on the strength of Marcus, who seemed to sleep on the seat beside her, carefully matching her breathing to the slow rise and fall of his chest. Grateful for the calm she had seen Marcus display more than once, she marveled that the greater the danger and chaos around them, the more centered and quiet the tall man became. To an observer, his body appeared to be totally relaxed, but Bright knew that he was like a cat, poised and ready to spring.

Watching him breathe from the corner of her eye helped her to focus and quell her terror at the danger surrounding them—danger to the silent eyes hidden in the forest on either side, danger to herself, to Marcus, and to the others in her care. Breathing in tandem with Marcus, silently she prayed for their safety, for courage to meet the responsibilities that rested with her this night, and then she prayed that the horses would not tire before they reached the English farm upriver.

"Do you want me to take the reins?" Marcus whispered, seeming to be inert, asleep, his lips almost still. From behind, the uniforms, more black than blue in the moonlight, passed single file and formed a cluster a few yards in front of them.

"No," answered Bright quietly. "I am in charge."

Marcus made no answer, but Bright sensed his acknowledgment.

The last of the uniformed men turned his horse abruptly around, causing Bright's team to rear. Struggling to control the horses and to keep the wagon upright, she was grateful as Marcus moved quickly forward to reach out and pull the reins, helping her to gain control.

"Where you headed, my pretty lady?" asked the soldier, sneering. "With a Negro in your wagon in the middle of the night? Be he slave? Or be he free?"

"Marcus belongs to my father," she said, working to keep her voice soft and steady. "We are delivering a load of rocks to stem a flood. Marcus has the responsibility of making sure I return to my father's farm safely. Here are his papers."

The man looked at the papers, shrugged, and handed them to his comrade. Bright realized that neither of the men could read, and she was much relieved.

"The papers look to be in order," said the first man, handing them back to Bright.

"We be looking for three Union deserters," said the other man. "Run from the Hungry River Union camp last week. You two sure don't fit that description. We ain't had no orders about slaves on the run. You wouldn't be a runaway slave, now would you?"

"Wouldn't no fool drive around with a runaway in her wagon in the middle of the night, anyways," said another man.

"If you see any uniforms or any brown faces around here," said the leader of the men, tipping his hat in Bright's direction, "you just send up a shot. We'll come a-running up here to help you, little lady, all the way from Pennsylvany, if need be." He spat a stream of tobacco juice into the underbrush growing on the embankment.

"Any brown faces or white faces, uniforms, anything, any day," said the other. "We'll come running."

"Thank you, gentlemen. I'll be sure to let you know," said Bright with a slight nod of her head, trying to keep the sarcasm out of her voice as she moved to cover her shaking hands with her cape. "*If* I need help."

Snapping the reins to urge the team back into the road as the horsemen broke into a gallop and rode on ahead of the wagon, Bright finally drew a deep breath and dared to look at the man beside her. He smiled and nodded in approval of her actions. She sighed in relief.

"Seen any Union soldiers? Deserters? Any brown faces?" asked Marcus quietly, still unmoving, but mocking the men with his voice, his face still, looking straight ahead. His eyebrows raised, his eyes dancing bright with moonlight as he looked away into a clearing lifted Bright's spirits. If Marcus could make light of the situation, then the danger must, at least for the moment, be past. Her father always said that Marcus had a gift for calming, and he did it most often by making light of the darkest situations.

To a watcher, she thought, Marcus would appear to simply be out for a drive, not facing threats to their lives and to the lives in their care. His pretense that all was normal comforted her, although she could not say just why it did so.

"Haven't seen many uniforms, but I have seen so many brown faces," said Bright, with a slight smile. "I wonder how many brown faces I *have* seen, slave and free."

"You and me, both," said Marcus, shaking his head in wonderment and pride. "A long line, we have both seen, no doubt."

Even without closing her eyes, she could see a long line of brown faces, those who had been part of her life over the past nine years. And she knew how that long line of faces had changed her.

CHAPTER 1 🌊

1853

THE FIRST TIME BRIGHT had seen a brown face, she had been six years old, so proud of being allowed to gather the eggs from the henhouse. She had gone alone into the small, dark log building her papa had built to protect the eggs from the fox that sometimes wandered into the yard at night.

She remembered that day. Inching her way through the pungent gloom so that her bare feet would not be soiled by the slimy piles the hens had left on the dirt, she had made her way to the row of bark baskets filled with straw. Bending over to pick up an egg, she saw something move in the corner of her eye. Two eyes had stared back at her from the darkness, eyes that belonged to something much larger than she was.

Dropping her basket and flinging her small body against the door, she sent it crashing against the log walls, its leather hinges torn.

"Papa! Papa!" she screamed. "Papa, come quick! The devil is in the henhouse!"

She could see her father wiping sweat from his face on an old rag as he turned to walk around the corner of the smithy shed. Jumping up and down, trying to curb the terror that raced her heart and made her neck cold with prickles, she said, "It is there. I saw it. With two big eyes very high near the wall in the corner."

"Why, Brightie, me lass," her father said, placing the hammer carefully on the anvil. "There be no deevil here on earth. Surely there be no deevil in our wee henhouse. Come, lass. What sort of man does this deevil appear to be?"

"No man," said Bright. "No person at all, Papa. Only two eyes watching me from the corner."

"Two eyes, ye say, lass?" said Papa. "Let us go have a look."

Removing his leather gloves, he knelt with one knee on the sawdust floor to welcome her. His tiny daughter threw both arms around his large neck, sinewy and strong from days at the forge. As he picked her up, she rested one hand on his arm just above his wrist. She touched the scar from a brand burned into his arm just above his hand—some very sad thing from his childhood, something of which he never spoke, even when she asked. Each time she touched the scar, it sent shivers up her spine, though the scar itself felt warm from the forge this summer day.

"He is there," she said, pointing. "The devil is there in our henhouse. I saw him." Her voice was muffled against her father's black hair as she squeezed her eyes tightly shut.

"Nay, lass," said her papa, placing one hand on the anvil to push himself to a standing position and lifting Bright to ride on his arm. Papa took a step toward the henhouse, but Bright screamed again.

"No, Papa, no! The devil will get us," she said.

"Now, wee Brightie, do ye no' think that your pa be a match for any deevil that could spook our poor henhouse?" He gently lifted her head away from his shoulder to look into her face.

Finally she opened her eyes to look up into her papa's blue ones, framed by dark brows raised in question of her. Bright had a thought that Papa's eyes and the summer sky behind him were exactly the same color. The corners of his mouth lifted into a smile. If Papa could smile, then Bright could smile, too.

"Tell me, lass," Papa said. "Shall I take me hammer to show him how strong I am?"

Bright nodded her head. "Yes." She thought Papa's hammer would be handy if he had to fight this devil. The circuit-riding parson only last Sunday had said the devil had great strength, but, she was sure, even a very strong devil was no match for her papa.

Taking long steps, Papa carried Bright and his smithy's hammer across the barnyard to the henhouse, past the garden patch, where Ma's cornfield beans wound around the cornstalks, almost ready to pick.

"What name shall we give this deevil?" Papa said, his lips now serious underneath his beard as he lifted the door to upright it and lean it against the wall.

"I do not know what name," Bright whispered, fear rising into her throat and causing her heart to race again. She closed her eyes and wrinkled her nose.

"But we must give this deevil a name, if we are to cast him out," said Papa, stepping over the high threshold and bending at the waist to enter the doorway. Bright drew closer to Papa's shoulder, fearing to peer into the dark corner again.

Then she heard Papa's voice, softer than she had ever heard it before in all her life: "No need to fear. No need to fear, my man. Make free."

Papa stood very still and silent, but Bright could feel the muscles in his arm grow tense and his heart beat more rapidly. Finally Bright lifted her head to stare into the darkness where she had seen the eyes. Papa's voice whispered again very softly, "Big Tom, as sure as I draw breath. Make free, my friend. Make free."

As she stared into the darkness, she could see the eyes, then she watched as a hand lifted to cover them while soft sobs broke the silence.

"Then it's not a devil, Papa?" whispered Bright, her lips close to Papa's ear.

"Nay," whispered Papa. "There. The man be safe for the time being."

Papa stood her on the floor and took Bright's hand in his. "Nay, wee lass. We have no deevil here. Only a poor man trying to make his way out of bondage. And we must give him a hand."

As they walked toward the house, he said softly, "And Brightie, me lass, we must no' tell a soul of the guest we ha' in our henhouse this day. No' a soul. Do ye ken, lassie?"

Bright nodded her head. "Yes, Papa. Not a soul."

And Bright had remembered her promise to Papa. She did not tell a soul about the eyes in the henhouse.

The following morning she woke to hear what she thought was a strange, deep voice speaking to her parents in the room below. She lay half asleep for a while, thinking over the events of the day before. Then she fell asleep again.

CHAPTER 2 ᴐ

1856

THE MAN IN THE HENHOUSE never returned, but Brightie remembered him clearly. Then one summer day when she was nine, as she carried a bucket of table scraps to the hog pen, she stopped to watch three mounted riders rein in at Papa's forge. Each of the men wore a holster with a pistol belted around his waist. One of the men carried a rifle, too.

Although Papa's forge was a busy place—as many drovers, tinkers, merchants, and stagecoaches passed on the plank road, now widened to become part of the Buncombe Turnpike—men wearing handguns were an unusual sight. Most of those who passed carried rifles in their wagons as protection for their herds or goods, but except for the occasional visit from the sheriff and his posse on their way along the road, pistols were rarely seen at the forge. They were a sight that always frightened Bright.

Straining to hear the harsh men's voices and Papa's soft answers, she waited.

"Slave run yesterday," the first man said. "We lost trace of him near the cliffs back there. Ain't no man alive can climb that sheer face. Perchance you have seen him hereabouts?"

"No slaves around here," Papa's voice said, as Bright prepared to dump the scraps into the trough. "Mountain farms too small to make slaves a paying proposition. My neighbors own no slaves, either. It would be easy enough to spot a black face here."

She had seen black people and brown people pass on the road, but such a face was an unusual sight at the forge. Then she remembered the man she had seen in the henhouse when she was six. She remembered Papa's words that day. *Was that man a slave?* she wondered.

Bright climbed on the lowest fence rail to pour the scraps into the trough. Squealing, the pigs jostled one another, splashing mud, each placing his front feet into the trough in order to claim territory and food. She watched as the hogs pushed the smallest pig into the background, where he could not reach the food.

"Poor fellow," said Bright, grabbing a long stick left from fence building. "I will help you." Poking the stick at the hogs, she tried to make a space for the smallest one, but the other hogs were stronger than she was. "Move over," she said, climbing to stand on a higher rail of the fence and pushing with all her might.

Then her foot slipped.

"Ouch," she cried, scrambling to maintain her balance while trying to keep her hands from the splinters in the fence post. Finally she grabbed the entryway Papa had cut into the boards for the hogs, thrusting her head inside the small shelter. As she did, she saw two eyes near the roof staring back. Surprised, she looked again.

She could see the outline of a man in the dim light inside.

She looked at the man more closely for a moment. Then the stench of the hogs reached her nose. She pulled her head out for air. She held her breath for a moment, then moved her head inside to whisper, "Hello."

She would have said more, but the man held his finger to his lips to silence her.

As she moved back out into the air, she pulled herself up so that she could look down the hill toward Papa's forge. The men were still there. They were looking for a black man. This man's skin looked brown in the dim light.

"They are looking for a slave," she whispered. "Are you a slave?"

"I am Marcus," the man whispered. "Go back to the house. Say nothing."

"I could lead you to the winter root cellar," said Bright, still whispering. "If you came out this way, the men could not see you. You are strong enough to roll the stone, I think."

"Go to the house, please, missy," said Marcus. "I know where the winter cellar is. Go, please."

"Then hide in the winter cellar. I will bring you some supper later," said Bright, climbing off, picking up the bucket, and running down the hill.

As she climbed the front steps to the porch, the men rode up the pathway from the forge.

"We need to water our horses," the first man in line called to Bright. She worked very hard to keep her eyes from turning toward the hog pen. She knew if she looked in that direction, she would show the men where Marcus was hiding. Then she had an idea.

"I could help you draw the water from the well," she said to the horsemen, smiling brightly. "I am very strong."

"And a pretty little 'un, too," said the man. "We can draw our own water, but we're grateful for the offer. How old ye be?"

"I am almost ten years," said Bright. "I help Ma in the house. I feed the pigs." She stopped, thinking that she should not tell the men this news. Then she hurried her words. "I help in the garden, and I am learning to milk the cows," she added breathlessly.

"Well, well, well," the man said, smiling.

Bright quickly dropped the bucket down into the well, filled it, and wound the winch to lift the bucket. When she had poured the water into the horse trough, Bright stood stiffly as the men led their horses to drink one by one. Afraid to walk toward the house, fearing their eyes might follow her to the hog pen or to the winter cellar, hoping that her words would not give away Marcus's hiding place, she did not know what to do.

When the last man had watered his horse, he reached into his pocket as he walked toward Bright. She was too frightened to move as he knelt on one knee beside her.

"I found this pretty stone back there a piece," he said, smiling. "I can pick up another for my little girl on the way back. This one's for you. You are a smart little lady."

Bright looked at the stone. It was pink and shining in the sun.

The man's voice startled her. "Have you ever seen a black man's face around this place, little lady?"

Bright swallowed and worked to keep her eyes from looking up the hill. She did not know what to say.

But she had a thought. He had asked about a *black* man. The man in the hog house had brown skin. "I have not seen a black man here," she said. "Sometimes they pass along the road. They seldom stop unless a wagon-wheel rim breaks or their horses need a shoe."

"She knows nothing," one of the men said as they turned to go.

Bright stood, clasping the stone tightly in her hand as the men rode away. She hoped Papa would be proud of her. She had not really told a lie.

Then she decided not to tell anyone that she had met this man named Marcus, not even Papa, at least until she could talk to the man again. She had many questions to ask him.

CHAPTER 3 ⌒

AFTER SUPPER BRIGHT CARRIED some corn bread dripping with butter, a roasted potato, and a fresh tomato wrapped in her apron to the winter cellar. Mama had gone to the forge to help Papa with the accounts, taking Bright's younger brother, Andrew, with her and leaving Bright all alone to work on her embroidery, a task she hated.

First she peered inside the hog house. Nothing there but hogs.

Then she walked to the winter cellar and made herself as small as possible to squeeze through the space between the stone used to cover the opening in winter and the entryway. The air smelled damp and earthy as her eyes grew accustomed to the darkness.

"Hello," she whispered. "The men are gone, Marcus. It is safe now. I have brought you some supper."

Silence. No answer came.

"I am Bright Freedom," she whispered. "Are you here, Marcus?"

Silence still.

"Marcus, I want to look at you," she said, stamping her foot. "Please come out."

A movement caught her eye, then a tall figure stepped out of the shadows.

"Missy." The voice was the same she had heard early in the morning in her parents' house so many years ago. "I be thanking you for keeping my secret. And for the supper. I will take it over here."

"I think I will stay while you eat," said Bright. "I want to ask you some things, some things I think you will know."

"Miss Bright," said Marcus, taking the food from her hands, "I think you should go back to the house. Your papa be some worried."

"He thinks I am working on my embroidery," said Bright, turning two crocks that Ma used for pickling vegetables in brine for winter use upside down. She sat on one of the overturned crocks.

"Sit down there," she invited Marcus, who shook his head, smiled at her, and sat on the ground in the shadows.

As he began to eat, she asked him why he was hiding at their house.

"I am acquainted with your papa," said Marcus. "Your papa and me used to work on a big farm together down the country. He make me safe here."

"Do not fret," said Bright. "Are you a slave, Marcus?"

"No longer, missy," said Marcus between bites.

"Papa told me all about slaves," she said. "He told me that my words could keep you from being free. Even when the man gave me the stone, I tried to be careful.

He asked me about a black man. He did not ask about a brown man. Are there other colors of men, too?"

"I have seen many colors," said Marcus, shaking his head again. "You be a right smart girl, just like your ma."

"I can read," said Bright proudly. "Andrew is learning. Papa says we are both smart. And he says we must read so that our rights cannot be taken away from us. Do you know why he says that, Marcus? He says we will learn when the time is right."

"Your papa is a man of his word," said Marcus.

"I think you and my papa are friends. I hear your voices speaking together early in the morning sometimes," said Bright.

"You do be right smart," said Marcus. "Yes, your papa and I have been friends for many years. I owe him my life and my freedom, the lives of my wife and others, too. And I believe that he owes me his freedom as well," said Marcus, staring into the darkness.

"Papa owes you his freedom?" asked Bright. "Was Papa not always free? What are you saying, Marcus? Was my papa a slave?" Her words tumbled over one another.

"Slaves come in all sizes and all colors in some places, missy," said Marcus, speaking slowly and choosing his words carefully. "Here and now, people like me be slaves. But white people been slaves in the past. Some are still slaves, though they are not called by that name. The Children of Israel were slaves of the Egyptians until Moses led them out of bondage. Yes, your papa was once bonded. But I reckon it be your papa's place to tell you his side of this story. You better ask him."

"All right, Marcus," said Bright. "I'll ask him. Will you tell me your side of the story? Please."

Marcus had finished eating. He sat looking at Bright

for a long time. "I be not sure what I should tell one so young," he said at last. "Nor what Tearlach, uh, Charles, would have you know, little one."

"I will ask him," said Bright. "I know you are Papa's friend because you know his secret name. Ma uses it only when all the doors are closed and only our family can hear. Now you tell me. How did you get to be a slave? Were you born a slave?"

Marcus continued to shake his head slowly. Finally, he spoke.

"I was born across the water," he began. "My papa was a leader, a chief like the governor of this state. I had slaves to wait on me. The enemies captured in war became our slaves. We lived where the sun always shone, where it was never cold."

Staring at the ground, his hands folded into tips under his chin, he continued. "Then one night, I awakened to hear our family screaming. I was some scared. My papa came running into the house where I lived. He picked me up and threw me out the window, shouting, 'Run. Run. Go into the forest.' "

Bright shivered, trying to imagine this tall man as a small, frightened boy.

Then Marcus continued. "I ran. As fast as I could I went, but men wearing face paint I had never seen caught me. One of them threw me over his shoulder. The next morning, we came to his village. He spoke to me, but I did not know his tongue. As I learned to do the hard and dirty work of his village, I learned to speak and understand his tongue. I was the slave of my father's enemies. The man who owned me made me work hard, but he did not beat me. From him, I learned that his people had killed my family."

Marcus stopped, coughed, and sat still. Bright felt very sad for him. She could not think of life without Papa, Ma, and Andrew. She reached out and took his large hand in her small one. As she did, she felt a scar on his arm, above the wrist, just like Papa's. The letters were the same. She patted the scar with her free hand and said, "I am so sorry."

Marcus only nodded, then he spoke. "I lived there for a few harvesttimes and grew to be a man. Then another people came in war to attack the village and killed my master. The winners of that war sold me to slavers. I was carried to a ship and shackled in leg irons. I was thrown into the hold of the ship with many others who did not speak my tongue. There was no one to tell me what was going on. The foul odor made my stomach heave. Everybody had the bloody flux. There was no water to wash and little to drink." Marcus stopped for a few moments, remembering the horrors.

Bright tried to think what such a life would be like, but she could not. Marcus continued. "For more days than I can count we tossed on the water, seeing the sky and breathing good air only when they made us walk on the decks. I prayed to die, but finally we reached some islands where it is warm all year, and we again stood on land. There, a new master came in his boat in the dead of night, bought us, and took us to Carolina to work on his cotton plantation. That was where I met your papa. He can tell you the rest."

"I want to know why you are here at our house," said Bright. "Will you tell me?"

"I think your papa will tell you that in due time," said Marcus. "But you must promise me that if you see me here, you must make like you do not see me. My life may depend on that."

"I will never tell," Bright promised. "For now you are my friend, too. I will tell Papa that I helped you to be free. I did not say the words those men wanted to hear."

"Your papa be some proud of you," said Marcus. "But you may well need to help me many times by speaking no words about me. Can you do that, little one?"

"I can do that," said Bright. "I did not speak of you today. Marcus, why do you have the same scar on your arm that Papa has?"

"We once belonged to the same master," said Marcus. "That is the master's brand, to mark us if we ran. Your papa, he would be hard to find. He looked like the other free men around us. I was easy to spot, but old Master, he branded us all the same. Said the scar would remind us of our place."

"Papa had a master, too?" asked Bright, remembering what Papa had said: "Even as I was not free."

"Your papa will tell you about it when he thinks you be ready," said Marcus. "Now you better be going back to your embroidery. Marcus got work to do." He stood and pushed against the rock that covered the entrance to make room for Bright to pass.

Bright held out her hand to Marcus. "We are friends," she said. "I would not say words that would take your freedom. I promise."

"We are friends, little one," said Marcus, shaking hands with her. "I trust you to keep our secret."

As she walked along the path to the house, she looked back at the stone. Yes, she would keep the secret until Papa was ready to talk about it. But now that

Marcus had told his story, she knew that being a slave must be terrible. Had her papa been a slave, too?

Running to meet Papa as he walked up the path toward the house, she hugged him and said, "Papa, I love you."

"I love you, too, my wee Brightie," Papa said softly, giving her a hug.

CHAPTER 4 ⌒

LATER THAT SUMMER, when the first hint of frost tinted the early morning, Andrew went to visit the boy his age on the next farm. Bright felt very lonely, although the forge was busy most of the day with wagons, harness, and tack to be mended. When her chores were done, she sat on the steps leading to the porch of the new clapboard house Papa had built—he was proud to show the world that he was a prosperous smith who could afford to use their old cabin as a summer kitchen to keep the heat and danger of fire out of the new house. She liked to watch the road—riders on horseback, wagons full of goods going to and coming from the Piedmont markets, and drovers urging their herds along—imagining the travelers' journeys and their adventures along the way.

Today she rested her chin on her fists and giggled as she watched a man and two boys struggle to march a flock of turkeys down the steep incline near the forge. The turkeys kept flying to rest on nearby tree branches while the boys chased them with switches in a vain attempt to keep the birds confined to the road. Bright thought the turkeys were the funniest travelers passing that day.

Then she heard Papa's voice. "Bright, what say you to a ride in the wagon over to Mills River today? The hired hand will see to the work of the forge."

"In the wagon?" said Bright. "To go with you? Oh, Ma, please let me."

"Charles, do you think you should take her?" asked Ma, bringing a bowl of peas to shell as she sat on the wide porch, shaded from the noonday sun. Bright noticed that Ma had grown very fat during the summer.

"Will do her good," said Papa, stepping outside and closing the door. "The fresh air. It be a healing grace, for more than one. Besides, Mairi, the pattyrollers will never be noticing a smithy and his pretty daughter on their way to mend the door of the brickyard's big oven."

"Do you think there be danger?" asked Ma, her face dark with fear.

"Less with than without," said Papa, quietly, to Ma. "I carry a wagonload of tools and the biggest of the bellows. Perhaps the cauldron for smelting, too." He turned to Bright. "What say ye, Brightie, my lass?"

"Ma, please." Bright looked at Ma, a plea as clear on her face as in her words.

"I'll be loading the wagon," said Papa. "Brightie, do your ma's bidding here in the house until I call for you to come climb on the wagon with me."

"I HAVE PACKED some noonday dinner for you and your papa," said Ma after she returned from the kitchen. "There is a bannock for each of you, and another for a visitor, in case you meet someone on the way." Ma handed her daughter a small woven bag and a basket covered with a clean cloth. "This night you will sup with the parson from the circuit. Then you will visit Aunt Vista's house for a few days."

"Who will stay with you, Ma?" asked Bright. She loved to go to Aunt Vista's house, where she had fried apple pies rich with butter at breakfast each day.

"Old Hannay, the herb woman, will come to stay with me this night," said Mama. "We will be very busy."

Taking Bright's hand, she walked with the child to the shed that covered the forge and smithy shop.

Papa wrapped the long wagon reins around the brake stick and climbed down to face Ma. Then he lifted Bright, swinging her around through the air, to place her on the wagon seat. She laughed. She had not grown too old to enjoy the feeling of flying through the air when Papa lifted her to sit in the wagon.

"All is in order," Papa said solemnly, leaning over to kiss his wife on the cheek. "The bundle is stowed securely. I shall be home on the morrow by nightfall. The repairs to the brickyard oven will take only a short time. Old Hannay will arrive within the hour."

"God keep you," whispered Ma, handing the rifle to Pa, who stored it within easy reach near his feet. Bright wondered why her ma looked as if she might cry. After all, it was a wonderful day, and Bright was going to ride in Papa's wagon all the way to Aunt Vista's house.

"And God keep you, my love, my Mairi," said Papa, climbing on the wagon spokes to his seat beside Bright.

"Bright," called Ma. "Keep your bonnet on. Your fair skin will burn easily. Wear your strings tied under your chin."

Then Papa snapped the reins and shouted in a loud voice, "Giddyap!"

The wagon seemed to leap, then pulled forward as the team strained to carry the heavy load. Papa's anvil, the bellows, the huge cauldron, and the shaping tools used by every smith, along with several filled toe sack bags, loaded the wagon.

As the wagon rumbled onto the plank road, Papa made a sound in his throat. It sounded like a mourning dove, Bright thought. From the laurel thicket above the house, a dove answered Papa's call. She tried to make the same sound, but she could not make her lips move in the same way. Later she would ask Papa to help her make the sound so that a mourning dove would answer her call, too.

Bright turned around to wave at Ma, who was standing beside the porch that bordered the front of their house. Ma waved, but Bright thought her ma's face looked more worried than happy.

"And now, me lass, would you be wanting to hear a tale of the auld country? Or do we sing a song, making our happy journey together?" said Papa, as they started up the small gravel road that led away from the turnpike.

"Tell me a tale," said Bright. "*And* sing me a song. Both, please."

She knew it was a happy day. She looked forward to spending the whole day, just her and her papa, together to sing and tell tales.

"Tell me how it is that you gave me the name *Bright*. Tell me of my birth," she said.

And with a broad smile, Papa winked at her and began to sing softly.

"On the day of your birth, the sun shone so bright
That your ma and I knew that the angels did light
all the skies to acclaim the wondrous birth
of the wee lass who came to sit by our hearth,
to live in our hearts and to brighten our days."

Bright grinned at her father. She liked this song, but she liked the chorus best. Papa lifted his head, a signal that she should sing with him. Her small voice joined his strong bass one as they sang.

"I will sing again of a place called home,
A place where bright freedom's song can ring with the bells
and sing through the skies,
a place of bright freedom, a place of all glory, a place of
bright freedom's song."

My goodness, thought Bright, *how I love my papa*. And the team clopped a rhythm on the stones of the road as Bright and her papa finished the song together.

"So Bright is the name of the bonny wee lass
who lives in our hearts and who brightens our days."

"Is that the truth of my birth?" teased Bright, when the song was finished. "Is that the truth? Ma tells me a different story."

"Oh, as Mairi tells the tale, you were named for her family, the good people who took me in when I first came up from the low country with naught but my skills as a smithy. The Bright family took me in and made me a part of them. Then they gave me the bonniest of their daughters to wife," said Papa, with great good humor in his laugh. "So, my wee lassie, if my good wife wants you to be named for her family, then that story it shall be."

"But is your story the truth, too, Papa? Ma says that sometimes two things can be true at the same time, and neither of them need be a lie," said Bright.

"And Mairi's tale is true, but my tale is true, too," said Papa. "The sun has never shone so brightly as it did on that day in December when you were born. I thought surely the angels were holding a mirror to magnify its brightness. I looked into your blue eyes. They were the color of the sky over the mountains that day. I touched the soft black curls that surrounded your face, and the brightness of my love for you almost blinded me."

Bright smiled and hugged her papa's arm.

"*Bright* had to be the only name by which you could be called, my child," said Papa softly. "And bright in my heart ye shall ever be." Taking the reins in one hand, he touched his daughter's cheek with his fingertips.

"And you shall be bright in my heart as well, Papa," said Bright, reaching out to touch the scar almost hidden by the cuff of his leather glove.

But her words were covered by the pounding of hooves on the road behind them. Turning around, Bright could see a group of horsemen riding hard behind them, with dust being kicked up all around them.

CHAPTER 5 ᕙ

"WHO ARE THOSE MEN?" she said, softly so that they would not hear her.

"They are horsemen, lass. Nothing more," said Papa, but Bright could feel the muscles in her father's hand tighten as he held the reins. She wondered why Papa might be fearful.

Papa moved the horses toward the edge of the narrow road, near to the embankment rising on one side, and the horsemen passed beside them. But the men slowed and finally stopped to wait for the wagon to reach where they sat.

Papa did not move. Bright could see the muscle in his jaw tighten slightly, but he kept the horses moving at a steady pace until he stopped in front of the group.

Bright peeked around her papa's sleeve to look at the men. One of them moved his hand to his hip to display a pistol. Each one, Bright thought, looked as if his face needed his ma to give it a good washing.

"Gude day, lads," said Papa, his elbows resting on his knees.

"Morning," said one of the men. "Who be ye? And where ye be headed?"

"Charles Cameron," said Papa, lifting his hat slightly from his head and then replacing it. "And my wee lassie, Bright. We be on our way to the brickyards at Mills River. I am a smith, as ye can see."

He lifted his arm and made a sweeping motion toward the wagon bed. "Word come yesterday that the door to the ovens has hinges that be almost worn through. The need of a smith is great, so I am on my way to make mends there."

One of the men moved his horse to lift the leather cover from Papa's hammers and bellows. He reached into the center of the wagon bed to give the anvil a ring with a knife hidden in his hand until that moment.

"Seems to be truthful," said the man with the knife to the others. "Looks like smithy's tools to me."

Bright did not like the men. She could tell that Papa did not like them, either.

"I be a man of truth," said Papa. "My farm is on Mairi Mountain off the Drover's Road, the Buncombe Turnpike, it is called, looking down toward the state of South Carolina. I am known by all around as fair, honest, and truthful. It is my reputation that I give a day's work for a day's pay."

"Raise sheep, too? Run hogs in the woods? Little farm on Mairi Mountain, smithy shop down the hill from your house, close to the plank road that's going down the mountain?" asked the man with the gun.

"That be our place," said Papa, smiling more broadly than Bright had ever seen him smile. "Named the mountain for my good wife, when I bought that piece of land. Howsomever, she was not yet then my good wife. I hoped the mountain's name being for her and all would help me with my suit. Seems it did: We be wed nigh on twelve years now."

Papa waited for the men to answer. Bright dared not move until Papa did, but her eyes darted from Papa's face to the faces of the men. She knew something was wrong. She could feel the tension in his body, but his words were spoken as if he might be bantering, only passing the time of day with a traveler at the forge.

Finally Papa took a breath to continue talking, but the man shook his head, saying, "Naming a mountain for a woman? What man would do a thing like that?"

"She must 'a' flummoxed him," said another, spitting tobacco juice near the wagon's wheels.

"Ye may be sure," said Papa, continuing in his bantering voice. Bright was confused by the difference between the teasing in his voice and the stiffness in his body. "She fair flummoxed me the first time I laid me eyes on that flaming hair. And when she spoke, I knew that naming a mountain for her was too little. But gentlemen, enough about my good wife. What be your business this fine day?"

Bright had been wondering the same thing.

"A man run night afore last, one from a big farm down the country, below the mountains. Plaquemens brought his slaves up from the rice fields to tend the wheat over at his place on Hungry River. They had no more than got here than one of them run. We are sent to catch him."

"We'll make that slave sorry he was ever born," said another of the men.

"Ought to be easy enough to spot," said Papa, moving his arm ever so slightly, as if to signal Bright to pretend that everything was all right even when she could sense it was not. "Not many slaves around here."

Her eyes widened, but she did not utter a sound.

"Few slaves about," Bright heard Papa's voice repeat. "Mountain farmers don't own slaves. Our farms are too small. A slave would be just another mouth to feed, even if we could afford the asking price of a good man."

"Seems to me one would be right handy for you, Cameron," said the man who seemed to be the leader. At least, Bright thought, he usually talked for all of them. "Being a smithy is might nigh a full day. Herding sheep seems like a full day, too. Then there's running that herd of pigs. You could use a good slave, it seems to me."

Papa chuckled, but Bright knew his voice was tense. "I take on Jim Adams's hired man when I need a hand. That way I be not beholden to feed him except during his work for me. Leaves more for my family to eat. Slave costs too much to keep."

The leader watched Papa's face closely as Bright saw a thin bead of sweat forming on his upper lip. Papa removed his hat and fanned his face.

"That sun be getting high in the sky," said Papa. "It grows summer-warm today. Good to talk, but I have work to do. And a child to deliver to her aunt's house."

Bright felt Papa's hand on hers, warning her again, urging her not to utter a sound.

The leader sat silently for a moment, as if trying to decide something. Then he said, "I've heard of him, this Charles Cameron. My uncle hired out some work to him. He looks like the smithy on Mairi Mountain. Let us waste no more time here.

"If you see a Negro on foot, send up a shot with that rifle," the man said, lifting his hat and turning his horse around.

"Good day, gentlemen. A man would be a fool to be risking his child, eh, lads?" said Papa. "I'll call for help if the need arises."

The men moved into the ditch to allow the wagon to pass. Bright peeked around Papa's arm to watch them leave.

"Are they hunting Marcus, Papa?" whispered Bright, when the men were out of sight. "Papa, I have seen Marcus and talked with him. I know he is your friend."

Papa continued to stare straight ahead. "Ah, my Brightie, so you know about Marcus." He spoke so softly that she had to lean toward him to hear. "Then we will have to keep that our secret. Marcus is a good friend. We dare not speak of it just now. The woods may have listening ears. Can you keep a secret, my Brightie?"

"I already have kept the secret, Papa," said Bright, feeling very grown-up, riding along beside her papa this fine day, keeping a secret that only Bright, Marcus, and Papa knew.

A FEW DAYS LATER, when Papa returned to Aunt Vista's to take Bright home, he told her another new secret. The news of a baby sister was so exciting that she forgot to ask Papa to tell her the story of his friendship with Marcus.

But when she remembered talking with the brown man in the winter root cellar, she was proud because she knew that her silence had helped him to be free.

CHAPTER 6 ✍

1859

THE YEARS PASSED, and the Cameron children grew, as children always grow. Bright was now twelve and feeling far more grown-up. The market road that ran all the way from Greenville, Tennessee, to Greenville, South Carolina, grew, too, as a greater number of wagon wheels and horses' hooves pushed back its borders.

Papa's forge grew busier and busier as more wagons, buggies, stagecoaches, and horses passed. Few days passed without a traveler coming or going to market and back, stopping at the forge for repairs, to pass the time of day, or to bring news from other places along the road. Finally Papa hired a farrier to handle the shoeing of horses while he took care of the business of the smith, making implements for farms and homes and repairing rims on wagon wheels.

The travelers who stopped at the forge spoke often of the prosperity that was coming to the mountain counties, and Bright listened whenever she took a pitcher of water down the hill for Papa and the farrier. She often overheard the men discussing the future of the railroad that was planned to link the town of Asheville to cities both east and west. The railroad, the men told Papa, would bring even greater prosperity to the mountain farms and businesses.

Once Bright had seen a locomotive, when she had gone to market with Papa. She remembered the noise of the great wheels, the hissing of the steam engine, and the sounds of the whistles. But she could not imagine adding that din to the sounds of the busy road that passed the forge. The traffic on the road made so much noise that, whenever possible, she escaped to the hills high above the house to tend the sheep or herd the cows, savoring the silence of the forest.

So many travelers came that Papa finally said it was necessary to keep a light burning beside the front door of the house every night. That way travelers would know that if their wagons or harness needed mending, they could knock to wake him.

Each morning Bright cleaned the lantern Papa had fashioned by rolling a piece of tin to form a lip to hold the wick where it dipped into fat left from cooking. Then she trimmed the wick made of scraps from Ma's loom and filled the lamp's well full to the top. Each night at dusk Papa carried a small branch burning with flame from the fireplace to light the lamp. As the light shone into the darkness, Bright listened for the sound of hooves passing, and of the few who traveled at night, only occasionally did anyone stop late at the forge.

Bright could hardly see a reason for keeping the lamp's light shining, but Papa insisted it must remain to welcome travelers. Once in a while a light knock could be heard. It was usually the Mennonite preacher from across the river. Bright watched from the window of her new room over the porch as Papa quietly opened the door and left. That preacher certainly needed a great many repairs to his wagon in the middle of the night, Bright thought. Sometimes she wondered why he did not come to the forge in the daytime like everyone else so that Papa could get some sleep.

Things were so busy at the forge that Bright and Andrew were given full charge of taking the sheep to pasture and moving them to new ground when the grass was nipped and too sparse to sustain them. Late each summer the sheep had to be brought down from the high summer pasture on top of Ivy Mountain and secured in a pen in the meadow behind the barn. There they joined the sheep bartered to Papa in exchange for farm implements or wagon repairs.

Then in the fall, she and her brother were busy rounding up the hogs given to Papa in trade by the drovers. The hogs had been allowed to roam in the woods all summer, feeding on acorns and other mast until they were fat enough to butcher and fill the smokehouse with hams, bacon, and side meat. The chickens, turkeys, geese, ducks, and guinea hens had to be fed and penned at night to keep them safe from the fox or wild dog that might wander by. When those tasks were finished, Bright and Andrew helped Ma tend the garden, digging the new potatoes to be stored for winter.

Any spare time Bright found was spent helping Ma with the house chores and playing with her sister, Peigein, now a curious little girl getting into everything within her reach. One afternoon in early autumn, Bright sat on the steps of the log cabin, peeling potatoes. She wondered how her family could eat so much food. It seemed that Ma was always cooking and washing pots.

"Ma, why are you cooking so many potatoes?" she called through the open door. "We can't eat so many tonight."

"We'll use them later," called Ma's voice.

"For soup?" called Bright. She loved Ma's potato soup with leeks in it.

"Mayhap," called Ma, coming out to join her daughter, her hair flaming in the warm sun. Bright thought her mother's hair matched the color of the maple tree with turning leaves near the smokehouse.

"Do you plan to open an inn?" Her daughter smiled at her. "You could take the business away from Sherrill's place."

"We could," said Ma, sitting on the steps beside her. "You never know who will stop, needing food, my daughter."

"Are we having visitors?" asked Bright.

"One never knows," said Ma, lifting Peigein up to sit on her lap, the small head nodding on her shoulder. Soon the child was fast asleep.

"Bright," said Ma, placing Peigein gently on the grass nearby, "chestnut stuffing would taste fine with the goose I'm roasting for supper. Papa's farrier tells me there are chestnuts ripening on the south side of the ridge. Would you like to go fetch some?"

Bright sprang to her feet. Gathering chestnuts was far more interesting than peeling potatoes. All alone in the forest, climbing the steep hillsides, searching for chestnuts—rich and brown as they rested in their sticky burrs—and eating her fill was, in her opinion, a fine way to spend an afternoon. Pulling her bonnet from the nail on the wall near the washstand, she quickly chose a basket from those hanging from the rafters and kissed her mother on the cheek.

"Watch for rattlesnakes," her mother called as Bright disappeared on the path that led behind the woodshed and around the contour of the hillside.

"I will take care," Bright called, eager to be on her way.

Climbing up the steep hillside and searching the ground for chestnuts in the afternoon's heat left her breathless, and finally she stopped to rest as the shade of the forest closed around her. Sitting on a huge log from a poplar tree long broken by age and wind, she removed her bonnet and fanned her face with a nearby tree branch. Closing her eyes, she listened. Only the sound of the wind through the pines and a faraway chickadee's call broke the silence. Soothed, Bright rested, allowing the sounds of the busy road to be washed away.

For some minutes she sat unmoving, until the sound of a sob broke her rest, a sob that came from the log on which she sat. Afraid to move, she listened again. Another sob. And then another sounded above the pines' soughing. Something was making a sobbing sound inside the log.

She stood slowly, quietly, and turned around. Walking as silently as she could to the end of the log, she leaned over to peer at the other side. It was dark, with dust from the rotting wood making a pool on the ground. The log was hollow.

Leaning down she looked more closely. A face, white with terror, seemed to be a part of the log.

"I won't hurt you," she said, reaching out her hand. "Who are you?"

The face shrank back, pulling into the darkness.

"I am Bright," she said. "What is your name?"

"Evie," the face whispered.

"Where did you come from?" asked Bright. "Let me help you."

"Is anybody else out there?" said Evie.

"No, I am alone," said Bright. "I will help you."

The girl crawled out, her clothing covered with wood dust and leaves. Bright was startled to see that Evie was about her age, perhaps a bit younger.

Sitting up, the girl said, "Do you have anything to eat?"

"Not much," said Bright, offering her basket. "Only a few chestnuts. Would you like some?"

Grabbing a handful of chestnuts, Evie stuffed them into her mouth, chewing them hulls and all, brown shells spilling from her mouth.

"You are starved, poor thing," said Bright. "My ma has plenty of food. Come down to our house, and we will feed you."

"I can't," said Evie. "I can't leave Lloyd. He might die."

"Who is Lloyd?" asked Bright. "Where is he?"

Evie watched Bright's face for a few minutes, as if trying to decide if she could be trusted. Then she said, "He be in the log, too. But he can't come out."

"He's in the log, too?" said Bright.

"He be hiding in t'other end," said Evie. "He can't let you see him. You might tell."

"Tell who?" asked Bright. "I am good at keeping secrets. I won't tell. My papa will keep him safe."

"Safe from my pa," said Evie, beginning to sob again.

"He be chasing us. Say he going to sell Lloyd downriver. Say we getting too big to play together. Say we can't be together now that I am a woman."

Bright shook her head. The skinny girl did not look like a woman yet. "Go on," she urged.

"Lloyd and me, we been together since we be born. My ma died, and his ma wet-nursed me. I lived with them in the quarters until last summer. Pa came to take me to his cabin. He be the overseer, and he say he need me to help him. I did not want to go, so I ran away back to the slave quarters." Evie sobbed between words.

"Are you a slave?" asked Bright.

"Me?" asked Evie quickly. "No. I be white like my pa. Lloyd be a slave. My pa say we can't be together no longer. So him and me, we run. And run. And run. And we be so tired and hungry. Lloyd found the log. He made me a nest in this end, and he crawled into t'other end."

Bright stood up and walked around the log. Stooping to look inside, she saw a dark face with two frightened eyes staring back at her. Reaching out her hand, she said, "Please come out. I won't hurt you. I want to help you."

The boy hesitated, then asked, "Be they anybody else out there with you?"

"No, I am alone," said Bright. "I will get help for you."

"I stay hid here," the boy said softly. "You take Evie to keep her safe."

Bright stood up and tried to think. It might be easier to take the girl to the house to Ma. Then she could return with Papa to get the boy. If the boy was a slave, Papa would know what to do.

"All right," she said. "You stay here. I will bring my papa to help you. He had a friend who was a slave. Take the rest of the chestnuts. I will bring food to you when I come back."

Taking Evie's hand, Bright led her down the hill to the house, where she found Ma in the kitchen, Peigein playing on the floor.

"Some men were here looking for them just after you left," Ma said. "We will need to hide her in the cave behind the root cellar."

"Cave?" said Bright.

"It's time you knew," said Ma, dipping potatoes and carrots from the pot and placing a bowl in front of Evie. The girl ignored the spoon Ma gave her and lifted the bowl to her lips, pouring the food into her mouth.

"You'll burn yourself," warned Bright.

"She's starved," said Ma sadly, and she filled the bowl again.

Handing two cold corn bannocks to Evie, Ma said, "We must hide you now. Some men were here a short time ago, looking for you. Eat these on the way. You must be very quiet. My husband will bring the boy to the cave as soon as it is dark."

She led the girls into the root cellar and struck a match to light a lantern Bright had never noticed before hanging on the shelves holding the harvest of apples, potatoes, carrots, and rutabagas. Pushing a board out of the way, Ma motioned for the girls to squeeze through a slim opening in the dank wall of earth. Then she followed.

Bright looked into the darkness that lay before them and saw clean straw lining the floor along the walls.

Ma hung the lantern on a stake in the wall and motioned for Evie to lie down.

"I will cover you with straw," Ma explained. "You

must be absolutely quiet, and stay right here until someone comes to take you out of here. Do you understand?"

"Yes, ma'am," said Evie, shivering.

Ma stuffed the straw around her for warmth and
stood to leave.

"It's dark," cried Evie as Bright and Ma blew out the
lantern and pushed through the opening into the root
cellar, leaving Evie alone in the darkness.

"It is dark," Ma told Bright. "And the poor child is so
frightened, there all alone. But we must hide her."

"Why, Ma?" said Bright. "She is not a slave. Her
friend is."

"She has helped a slave escape. And she went with
him. Her father will be almost as hard on her as he is on
the boy," said Ma as they came into the sunlight again.
"We must do what we can to protect them. I only hope
she can stay in the darkness alone."

Bright shivered, remembering how dark and damp
the cave was. "Shall I tell Papa?" she said.

"I will tell him when I ring the supper bell," said Ma.
"The boy is safer under cover of darkness. Now it is time
for milking the cows. Your papa sent Andrew to the mill
this noon. He is not yet returned. We must go on about
our business as if the boy and girl were not here."

Bright gathered the pails from their pegs and took
some clean white cloths sunning on the side of the
springhouse, where she had hung them after cleaning
them this morning. Then she went to the corncrib to
pour shelled corn into the bucket for the cows to eat
while she milked them. Ma said they tricked the cows
into standing still with the corn.

At the milk gap, Bright began her chores by pulling
one end of each of the four long boards Papa had used

to build a gate, laying each on the ground. Then she placed the pails inside the pasture. Finally she returned the boards to keep the cows from getting into the garden patch and making their way into Ma's flower beds. Three of the cows were there waiting patiently at the gap for the corn, but the other was missing.

"Soo, cow," called Bright cheerfully as she poured corn into the trough. "Soo, cow." But the cow was nowhere to be seen.

As she worked, Bright thought of Evie all alone in the cave in the dark. And of Lloyd, hiding inside the log in the woods. She had wished so often that she could help those who were like Marcus. Now she had a chance to help someone to be free. Someone her own age, she thought, would be free because of her. This thought gave Bright one of the best feelings she had ever had. She smiled and began to sing Papa's song about the day she was born softly to the cows.

From the direction of the brook Bright heard dogs barking and the sound of rough voices shouting. Probably the sounds of the road, she thought, but it was usually quiet up here in the pasture.

When she had finished milking, she tied a clean white cloth over each pail and set it on the side of the fence away from the cows. Then she went to search for the missing animal. The dogs were still barking, their voices growing fainter each moment. After she found the cow, perhaps she would see what all the noise was about.

Pushing the needles of thick pines aside, she walked carefully on the muddy earth bordering the brook, her feet sinking with each step. Finally she saw the cow standing beneath a large oak tree with limbs that stretched out over the water.

"Soo, cow," she called softly. The cow ignored her, so Bright moved closer.

Someone was lying on the ground. He was dressed in the faded linsey shirt and pants of a poor farmer. Or a slave.

"Hello," she called, but the person did not move, so she stepped across the brook on the rocks that formed a path through the water.

Moving closer, she could see a face. Or what was left of a face. The black hair was covered with blood. The dogs she had heard, or something, had torn at the face and neck, just like the wolves that had killed several sheep in the high pasture last year had done.

Then Bright realized—it was Lloyd, the slave she had left hidden in the log. For a moment her feet were frozen, her mind a jumble. Her stomach felt as if the dasher on Ma's churn were inside it. She turned and ran, screaming, mud pulling her at every step until she reached the milk gap. Stumbling, she climbed over it, spilling the pails of milk, and ran down the hill toward the house, her legs pumping and her heart pounding in her ears.

As she came in sight of the forge, a group of men were riding away, one of them driving a wagon. Ma came walking quickly toward her.

"Bright," she said quietly, nodding toward the men, "don't say a word. Come with me to the house."

"I found Lloyd," gasped Bright as Ma drew her into her arms, comforting her. "The dogs have torn him . . . We must help him."

"I know. I know," said Ma. "The men came down the mountain a few minutes ago. They left him for dead. They are still looking for Evie."

Bright could not speak. She gasped, trying to form

words between her sobs. "Lloyd's alive, but he's hurt." She stopped for breath. "And where is Evie?"

"She is safe for now," said her mother. "I was so fearful of this. Papa will bring Lloyd down to the house. We will take care of him. You have done all you could."

"But I didn't," sobbed Bright. "I could have brought Lloyd to the cave with Evie. Now those awful men have almost killed him. And it's all my fault."

"No, my Brightie," said Ma, soothing with her voice. "It is the fault of a way of thinking in which Evie's papa loves his sick beliefs about his fellow humans more than he loves his daughter. He turned the dogs loose. You had nothing to do with that. You behaved with great courage and with great kindness. You cannot do more. Let us go get your papa. We must help that boy."

The back door to the summer kitchen opened softly. Bright looked up to see Marcus standing there, his face drawn in pain.

"I brought the boy down from the pasture," he said. "He is with the girl in the cellar. I need some water and rags. Do you have some of Hannay's salve, Mairi?"

"Bright, fill the bucket with hot water from the kettle," said Ma, searching the pantry for the tin of salve, then handing Marcus both the tin and a brown bottle. "Bring the rags from the shelf. And here is a bottle of tincture to help ease the pain for the boy. I will be along shortly."

Bright followed Marcus from the kitchen and watched as he crossed the short distance from the door to the winter cellar in three long steps. Inside it was damp, dank, and dark. She could hear Evie sobbing as Marcus lit the torch in its holder on the wall.

In the cave, Evie rocked back and forth as Marcus

knelt beside the boy and began to clean his face. He handed Bright the blood-soaked rags to rinse. Twice she returned to the kitchen for more hot water, but Ma was no longer there. Bright wondered where she was, but took no time to search. Marcus needed her help, so she must not tarry.

As soon as she knelt beside Marcus again, the stone rolled away from the cellar's entrance, allowing the last rays of the sun to enter the gloom. Pa and Ma walked hand in hand, their faces drawn and sad.

"Pa," Bright began, standing.

"I know, my Brightie," he said, sadly. "I know. We must get them out of here before the men realize they are hiding. The wagon is ready. The sun is almost gone."

"Can the boy travel, Marcus?" asked Ma, kneeling to tear cloth into strips and help Marcus make bandages to cover the worst of Lloyd's wounds. "I will give him herbs to help him sleep. Old Hannay knows what she is doing."

Papa helped Evie to her feet. "You must be brave if you are to keep the boy safe," he told the girl. "Can you be very quiet and still when we hide you under the load of hay?"

"Can I breathe?" she said.

"Yes," said Papa. "The hay is loose. Plenty of air will get in."

"Then I must help Lloyd. He is my best and only friend. Oh, how could my papa be so mean?" Evie began to cry.

Ma walked over to place her hand on the girl's shoulder. "We don't know, honey," she said, comforting the girl. "Some things are very hard to understand. But, right now, we must get you and Lloyd to safety."

As soon as twilight crept across the valley, Papa

brought the wagon, loaded high with hay, to the front porch. Bright and Ma walked with Evie, helped her to climb into the wagon, and covered her with hay.

Papa and Marcus carried the sleeping boy through the summer kitchen, across the hallway, and down the front steps. Marcus climbed up to lie in the wagon, his head very close to Papa's back. He held a rifle. Papa covered him and the boy with hay and climbed to the wagon seat.

To Bright's great surprise, Papa did not say good-bye, but slapped the reins quickly and urged the team into a fast trot.

"They are so young," said Bright. "Younger than I am."

"And in so much danger," said Ma, hugging her daughter. "I only hope our men can reach the Mennonite's house before Evie's papa realizes Lloyd is still alive and his daughter is gone."

"They are so young," Bright repeated, as the wagon rolled out of sight into the darkness covering Mairi Mountain.

CHAPTER 7 ◈

LATER THAT NIGHT, after Marcus and Papa had returned to the house, Ma made cups of strong tea to drink as they sat in front of the fire. Bright was allowed to stay up with the adults. She was afraid to go to bed, for each time she closed her eyes, she could see the young boy torn and mangled.

"He would have turned loose the dogs on his own little girl, his own flesh and blood," said Ma, her voice stiff with pain. "How can a human be so cruel?"

"She helped a slave to run," said Marcus. "And, worse, she ran with him. To her pa, in his position as overseer of slaves, that disgrace is worse than her death would have been. To get the boy, he would kill his own daughter. Things grow worse and worse. Our work grows more dangerous each day. But we must push on."

"And it is time that Bright knew about the work," said Ma. "We can't keep it from her longer. This afternoon she became a part of it."

"But Mairi," said Papa. "We must protect her."

"She knows enough that we cannot protect her unless she knows everything," said Marcus. "Bright can keep our secrets. I know." And he smiled at her. "She has kept my secrets for years, haven't you, my little friend?"

His words made Bright feel better. Yes, she had kept all the things Marcus had told her as secrets.

"Then you agree it is time?" Papa looked inquiringly at Marcus.

"It is time," said Marcus. "Don't you agree, Mairi?"

Ma nodded. "It will be easier than having her ask questions," she said, picking up her carding combs and a handful of wool and beginning to prepare the soft fibers for spinning into thread.

"Our work," said Papa, "is to help any who would escape their bondage to find the freedom that is each man's right."

"And each woman's, too," added Ma.

"Yes," agreed Papa. "We do that by making any who walk the long road to freedom welcome with food, warmth, and safety until a guide comes to lead them on. Our work be secret except for a few others who do the same work in this county and those nearby. We only know those who help us directly with the bundles . . ."

"Those who are carried to freedom are referred to as *bundles*," Ma added. "Since all supplies to the forge arrive in bundles, and the plows and cook pots Tearlach makes leave the forge in bundles, too. The word is used for everything that arrives and leaves from the forge."

"Beyond our mountains, there are others who give aid, but we do not know them. We write no records. We leave no trace, for the safety of all those involved," said Papa. "And Marcus, here, is the guide who risks his life to help others to safety even as he risked his life to give me mine."

"And you have risked your life many times to keep me in safety, my friend," added Marcus.

"But how could all this be going on here?" said Bright.

"You have been busy with the games of a child, as Andrew is even now," said Ma. "The activity and noise of the forge and the road cover much of the activity and sound of our work. And, recently, you have been helping me with the work. Peeling potatoes is a very important task when starving travelers are to be fed."

Bright was confused. People had been coming and going at her home, and she had never noticed. So many things she did not understand suddenly made sense.

"Then the lamp is not for travelers, is it?" she asked.

"For travelers? Yes," Papa answered. "But not the travelers who use the turnpike. The ones who enter a cave near the roadway down the mountain a piece and make their way to our root cellar. The secret travelers who travel the underground path beneath our farm."

"But how do they know where to come?" asked Bright. "Who tells them?"

"Word spreads to those who need to know," said Marcus. "The boy and girl you met today were trying to reach this place of safety."

Bright felt her eyes filling with tears. She placed her teacup on the table and hid her face on her folded hands. She began to cry softly.

"Brightie," said Papa, patting her shoulder tenderly, "this day has been one of sadness and woe for you. But this day you have grown into a young woman. You have become a part of our work. I would have had you wait until you were older, but we do not always choose these things."

Then Bright raised her head. "Marcus, you said Papa would tell me his story when it was time."

"Brightie remembers everything, just like her pa," said Marcus. "She never forgets. Yes, Tearlach, I think it is time, don't you?"

"Tom, what have you told my Brightie already?" asked Papa.

Bright looked from one man to the other. "Who is Tom?" she said. "I know Tearlach is Papa's secret name. Do you have a secret name, too?"

"As my name in bondage was Tearlach, my friend's name was Big Tom," said Papa. "When a man leaves bondage behind, he needs a new name to celebrate his freedom."

"He needs a new name so those who would take him back into bondage cannot trace him," added Marcus, his voice sharp. "That might be a more important reason."

"Now, Papa, tell me your side of the story," insisted Bright. "If I am old enough to be a part of your work, I am old enough to know everything."

CHAPTER 8 ∞

"WELL, WHERE DO I BEGIN?" asked Papa. "Do you recollect the tales I have told you about my boyhood in the auld country, the land of the Scots?" he said, taking his curved pipe from the mantel and preparing it.

Lighting it, he puffed contentedly and began his story.

"You recollect that I told you how we were removed from our croft at Hornival on the Isle of Skye. Our land-lords wanted to be rid of us. I had been an apprentice to the village smithy. The smith in a small village is a very important man. But one day, my master up and died."

Bright was sure she could hear the keen disappointment in her papa's voice as he continued.

"Then one day the emigration man came to say that our grazing rights were null. We would be forced to leave the land we had lived on all our lives."

Bright felt a lump in her throat.

"We were rounded up," Papa continued, "and taken on foot along the coast all the way to Liverpool to be placed on ships bound for Australia. We learned to speak some English along the way. My family was held at a boardinghouse until we sailed. But I was awakened one night to find my hands tied and a dirty rag in my mouth. I was what they called kidnapped."

Papa stirred the fire and threw on more wood, then he continued. "I was carried to a ship and shackled in leg irons. Then I was thrown into the hold with many others—all ages, sizes, and kinds. The odor was most foul from the bloody flux. No water to wash, nor even much to drink on board. For more days than I can count, we were tossed around, little room to lie down and not enough height to stand. The leg irons chafed my legs. Many's the day I prayed to die, like so many of those around me."

Bright watched her papa carefully. Then she said, "That sounds like what you told me long ago, Marcus. It sounds like what happened to you."

"Bondage is bondage," said Marcus. "Many of us, people of all colors, reached these shores in chains. Yes, Brightie, your papa's story and mine are much alike. All the horrors the slavers used on us they had already practiced on their neighbors, or so it seems."

Then Papa said, "One day the captain brought me to the deck and placed a paper in my hands. He told me to sign an X, and with that X, I signed my life away."

"How sad, Papa," said Bright.

"But remember, my Brightie, that I am here now a free man helping others. How I got here is the story," Papa added, shaking his head. "It was seasick as a dog I was. The close air of the hold and the stench there made my sickness worse. Then the captain learned I had skills as a smith and brought me up top. The fresh air on deck gave me a reason to make an effort to stand.

"As I made repairs around the ship, the navigator, also a Scot, offered to teach me to read, to write, and to cipher," Papa continued. "For the rest of the journey, we worked evenings, him teaching and me learning. By the time we reached harbor, I could make my way through the Bible with little help, and I could write so's it could be read. I could tot up a column of figures so's I didn't get cheated. If I had been able to read when we sailed, I would never have signed the paper the captain of the ship offered, and he could not have sold me into servitude.

"But the captain put me on the block where we docked on the islands, an auction for bonded whites, down along the wharves near the black slave market. He sold me into a ten-year bondage to a rice farmer to pay for my passage," said Papa. "And that man sold me, just as the slaves were sold, to a man who brought me to Carolina."

Bright spoke, her voice fearful, "Were you a *slave*, Papa? Is that the reason for the scar on your hand?"

Papa was silent, and when he spoke, his voice was filled with sadness. "A slave like Marcus? No. I had *some* hope of being free. The men of darker skin who worked alongside of me would never be free. But it would only take me ten years to earn my freedom." Shaking his head, he added, "Or so I thought. And yes, the branded scar was a part of that servitude." As he usually did during deep thought, Papa began to trace the letters on his hand with his other hand.

Marcus was staring into the fire, tracing the letters burned into his arm in tandem with Papa.

CHAPTER 9 ∽

"WHAT HAPPENED, PAPA?" asked Bright. "Why did they brand you? Did it hurt? Did they burn your hand?"

"Yes, our arms were burned with a hot iron. At the end of my indentureship, I asked for my freedom, but my master told me that my papers were not legal, that I owed him seven more years. That was about the time he thought to brand us so that if we ran he could find us. A black man's face was easy to spot, but my face looked like everyone else in any town. So he branded each of us with a hot iron, using the initials from his name to mark us, a mark that we would wear for life."

"Those were dark days for your papa," said Marcus. "And for all of us in the quarters."

"Yes," agreed Papa. "With the brand and another seven years' indentureship, I had little hope. And when times were hard, I learned that my value to the master was less than the value of Marcus because he had paid much money for him. When food was scarce, Marcus shared his with me. Most of the indentures on the place died, many from starvation. I lived because of my friend. And unbeknownst to me, Marcus would be the man who would also bring about my freedom."

"Thank you, Marcus," said Bright. "Thank you for helping my papa."

"On the plantation there was only one other indentured servant still living when the massacre happened, a yeoman boy from England, one Edward Bailey, a cooper," said Papa. "He and Marcus were my good friends. Big Tom later became Marcus, Brightie. He was the leader of the slaves, like a preacher. Why don't you tell her what happened next, Marcus."

Marcus stared at the fire as he began. "The master beat an old grandmother for refusing to tell him where her son had fled. I could not control the others. They refused to listen to me. While I was asleep, some of them went into Master's house and killed his family. Then they set the house on fire. Their shouts awakened me. There was nothing I could do. If I ran, I was sure to be caught. But your papa, he had a chance to get away."

"So Marcus brought a small sack of food and said, 'Make free. Make free. I will say you tried to save the master and died in the attempt,' " added Papa. "So I ran and I ran. Young Edward ran, too. I owe Marcus both my life and my freedom."

Bright reached out to pat the scar on Marcus's arm.

"By the time I reached the Blue Ridge Mountains, I heard that Tearlach Cameron had died in the fire. So one Charles Cameron made his way here. Caught in a rainstorm one day, I found a cave and lived in it some days. By the winter's snows, I knew that the cave had many branches under this mountain. That day I vowed to claim the land one day and help others to freedom in any way I could."

"Then he made his way to my door," said Ma. "I knew he had been indentured when I saw the brand on his arm. So I fed him and asked my mama if he could stay."

"By the time I finished the biscuits Mairi made for me that day, I knew that one day we would be wed." Papa smiled and took Ma's hand. "When I learned this land had no claim on it, I registered this mountain as Mairi Mountain. Then I felled the trees to build a cabin, and we were wed."

Bright turned to Marcus. "How did you get your freedom?" she asked.

"It was a long time coming," said Marcus. "My wife was sold downriver when times grew hard. Then I was sold to a farm closer to the mountains. I had heard of a smithy named Cameron on Mairi Mountain, a big Scot with a pretty red-haired wife. I knew if I ran, he would do for me whatever he could. And one day, I made it to the mountain and hid in Cameron's henhouse, where their pretty little girl—"

Bright interrupted him. "You were running away when I found you in the henhouse!"

Marcus chuckled. "Brightie, that 'deevil' in the henhouse was old Marcus."

"If Papa had told me," she said blushing, "I would never have called you a devil."

"Charles and I have often repeated the tale of that day," said Marcus. "As scared as I was, remembering you as you ran to your papa makes me smile. Anyway, with help from Charles and others like him, I made my way through the mountains to Ohio, then on to Canada."

"There Marcus educated himself, married, and has a new family," added Ma. "But he returns again and again to help us in the work. He guides many on their way to freedom. We are only his helpers."

"And now you know all the stories from Marcus and from me," said Papa. "Today you saw the dangers of our work, long before I had hoped you would know. And now you are a part of our work. Are you ready, my bairn?"

As BRIGHT DRIFTED INTO SLEEP, she kept sitting up, startled, seeing the boy the dogs had attacked on Mairi Mountain that day. Then she ordered herself to put the images away until she needed them to remember her papa and Marcus and what bondage meant. And she vowed to do everything in her power to carry on the work of her family. Everything.

CHAPTER 10 🌀

1860

DURING THAT YEAR, after Bright helped Mama feed any bundles newly arrived and send them on their way, when the farm chores were finished and the household work was done, she would go down to the forge and work on Papa's account books, keeping the charges and the payments in her neat handwriting.

Bright had begun to look more like a young woman than a child, and the drovers who stopped by the forge for the services of the farrier Papa hired had noticed. Although none ever spoke his admiration of her when she appeared in the doorway to ask her father a question, she was aware of the new praise in their glances. She rather liked that they noticed. It made her feel very grown-up.

Except on the warmest days that summer, she sat out of the way just inside the small lean-to her father used as a storage shed and office to keep his account books. She liked listening to the men and their talk of politics and the wonders from the world beyond their mountain, with news gleaned from the newspapers they brought back from the Piedmont towns.

Sometimes she paid attention to gossip from nearby farms and villages, but she found that talk less interesting than all the words she heard about *slaves*. And almost everyone who stopped at the forge these days talked about slaves, whether they owned slaves or not, what they cost, what caused them to run, and what could be done about their running away.

And so she listened, gathering her thoughts and adding every new piece she heard to the puzzle inside her head. She had heard talk of the fugitive slave law that had made the work of her papa and Marcus more dangerous, the Kansas-Nebraska Act, the Wilmot Proviso, and the Compromise of 1850, all of which were supposed to settle the issue but had apparently only made some states enemies of others.

She listened, but more and more she disagreed with many of the speakers who visited the forge. At first she had argued with Papa at supper that he should speak his views about slavery and tell those who disagreed that he knew what bondage was like. But Papa had told her that the thoughts and opinions of his family had no place in the work of the forge. They were there to do a job and do it well. To state his opinions to those who had business at the forge might endanger the work and their family, he reminded her. Silence was the only way to keep the family safe.

And so Bright kept her opinions to herself until the family was alone inside the house. At the forge she often found herself so angry she had to turn her thoughts to the figures on the page and pretend not to hear. Sometimes Bright wrote down the new words she heard in the margins of Papa's accounts so that she could ask at supper what they meant.

As the days passed, it seemed that those who visited the forge could talk of little else but war and slavery. Sometimes a man who came from the Piedmont towns would leave a newspaper for Papa. He and Ma would take turns reading it aloud when the supper dishes were washed. Then they would talk about the events from the cities.

"I hear more and more talk of the problems of slavery," said Papa. "I fear we will come to a fight over it." He shook his head sadly.

"Surely not," said Mairi. "Surely a compromise will be found."

"Each and every compromise so far only aggravates the issue," said Papa. "This practice of enslaving others be a scourge on mankind. It brings about loss of life where none should die, like Lloyd and Evie, the young ones."

"Lloyd and Evie?" said Ma and Bright at the same time.

"Yes," said Papa, sighing. "We carried them to safety. The boy's face healed. But he and the girl ran again without a guide. This time, her father caught them. They are both dead. The tinker brought word from Banner Elk this day." Papa paused, looking down. "Such news saddens the heart."

Bright's throat tightened, and she felt as if she were choking. She needed air. Leaping to her feet, she ran out the door, slamming it.

Evie. Lloyd. They were even younger than she was.

And they were dead. Despite the efforts of her papa and Marcus, they were dead. Despite the healing salves Ma had applied to Lloyd's face, they were dead.

They would never feel the cool night air on their skin again. Or smell the fragrance of honeysuckle. Or taste the buttered crust of a fried apple pie.

Falling to her knees beside the well, she reached for the dipper and poured water over her face and hair, sobbing as the chill startled her.

Then Papa's hand warmed her shoulder as she heard his voice. "Ah, Brightie. Sometimes life be as hard as stone. This thing be hard, so hard as to break the heart."

Bright thought Papa was right about that.

CHAPTER 11 ⁊◌

ONE WARM DAY THAT FALL, Bright sat darning Papa's socks on the house porch as Andrew helped their father round up the sheep. She loved to watch the sheep—white-faced Herdwicks with their gray fleece, and the Suffolks with their black faces and stocky bodies—running back and forth across the barnyard making ever-changing patterns.

Andrew was fast on their heels as Billean, their golden collie, a gift from Morgan the tinker, nipped and barked at the animals, separating them. Papa said that Billean had the makings of a fine sheepdog.

Papa gathered the young ewes and a few almost-grown lambs into one group to be penned for the coming winter's food and for spring breeding. Then Andrew and Billean herded those selected to go to market into a stockade near the turnpike, to wait until it was time for the journey to begin.

Ma stood guard at the vegetable garden, Peigein clinging to her skirt. Most of the plants were already browned by first frost, come early that year to the top of Mairi Mountain.

Bright placed her mending on the step and stopped to stroke her little sister's cheek before she lifted the last of the food and gear from the porch to be loaded on the wagon. They would camp along the way for the ten days' journey to the market and back. Moving the sheep was a "slow go," as Papa had told them. They would need to show patience, for the animals had short legs and could only move so fast.

Bright remembered when she had last been allowed to go to take a herd of pigs to market one autumn when she was small. But this year she would take the responsibility of a woman. After all she was almost grown.

At last Papa grasped the horns of a big ram and moved him slowly into the stockade. The stragglers followed, with Andrew and Billean rounding up those that strayed from the herd.

Papa checked the oxen's harness and secured the double-tree that kept the wagon from running over the oxen's rear hooves when they traveled down steep hills.

"Brightie. Andrew. Do we be ready to push off?" he called, walking over to give Ma last-minute instructions and hug her and Peigein one more time.

Ma had reached up to touch her husband's face when the neighbor's hired hand came dashing through the woods. He quickly pulled off his hat and made a slight bow toward Ma.

"A bundle will be delivered to your door this dark. It is in need of repairs. Master Adams sent me to tell you it is on the way. That is, if you will receive it. Marcus will call for the bundle by sunup," he said breathlessly, his words running together.

Ma looked at Papa and drew in a deep breath. He waited for her to speak.

"We will receive it," she said finally. "We will repair it, but we must count on Marcus to take it on its way for we have no way to carry it on to its receiver this day. Is he hereabouts?"

"Master Adams told me to say that you need only receive the bundle. Marcus will take it from here. He knows of your market plans, Master Cameron," said the hired man.

"Will you be welcoming it, with me not here?" Papa asked Ma, his face worried.

"I will always be welcoming a bundle," she answered. Then she turned to the hired man and said, "Is this bundle large or small? Does it fit man, woman, or child?"

"Master Adams asked me to say that the bundle fits woman and child," the man replied. "As soon as it is mended, Marcus will take both to the Mennonite preacher to deliver it further."

"Tell him that we will secure the bundle," said Ma, turning back to her husband. "Now, Tearlach, dearest, be on your way. I will be as safe with Marcus on the place this night as if you were here yourself. He will return here when his responsibilities are finished, if need be. I will care for all on this place until your return."

The hired man turned and ran, lost his hat, and ran back to get it. As he rounded the curve in the road, he was carrying his hat in his hands.

Andrew and Bright laughed.

"Make sure the corncrib and the root cellar be secured. We have the winter's crops therein," said Papa. "Most of all, make sure that you be safe, Mairi." His voice was soft and tender. "Do you choose to do this? With Marcus as the carrier?" he added.

"I am sure, dear Tearlach," said Ma with a smile. "You take a care with our wee ones and your own self."

Bright and Andrew looked at each other in disgust. They hardly considered themselves to be wee ones.

Papa and Andrew herded the animals down the steep incline of the market road as it wound around the mountainside, while Bright drove the oxen and wagon behind them. The slow pace of the animals and the rocking of the wagon wheels grinding against the stones in the roadbed gave Bright time to think.

Papa, Mr. Adams, and the hired man had spent much of the winter last year building a new corncrib and a wagon platform to adjoin the forge. Then they spent the rest of the spring days digging a large cellar under the platform.

All winter Bright had watched the men building the corncrib and the platform, stopping to look from the window as she helped Ma with the housework. She watched even more carefully as the men hauled away the soil from the area under the center of the platform, leaving a space for her father to stand upright under a wagon. Placing a line of stones on each side at the top allowed the wagons to be rolled backward on the platform even in the mud. Building a roof and sides to protect the platform made repairs possible in any kind of weather.

Bright thought that few who visited the forge knew the reason for the changes in the wagon rack or about the tunnel that linked the root cellar, the corncrib, and the long cave that opened far down the mountain. Papa spoke often of the speed with which he could now finish his smithy's work. Marcus appeared and disappeared like a shadow, and often spoke in the firelight of the added safety of the arrangement at the forge.

Bright was very pleased that, each day, she helped to feed the bundles, helped to brew the herb tea that caused the small children to sleep so they would not be heard, and helped Ma knit mittens and caps from the wool shorn from the Cameron sheep. Many of the slaves arrived and departed barefoot, even in the snow, so stockings were of little value.

Yes, she was very proud of her part in the work. She knew she was part of something larger than her small place on Mairi Mountain.

CHAPTER 12 ⁊⊙

THE HUSTLE AND BUSTLE of the stockyards made Bright's head spin with excitement. Papa led the way into the auction area, where farmers from three states brought their livestock to be traded. A rail siding nearby, with a locomotive hissing steam and puffing occasional belches of smoke, allowed the buyers from larger cities to load the stock they bought and send it on its way.

Taking off her bonnet, she fanned herself. The weather had grown steadily warmer as they had descended the mountain. The humid heat was oppressive, and there was only a faint breeze stirring the leaves over her head. She longed to be home on the mountaintop, where it was cooler.

The heat made her sleepy, and she dozed, dreaming of her papa in chains tossing on the big ship that carried him over the ocean. She was sleeping soundly when she heard voices coming from behind the tree against which she was leaning.

"I treat my slaves well," said a strange man's voice,

almost shouting. "I feed them. I care for them. I don't beat them. I don't sell them away from their families."

"You are a fool, Edward. You want slaves to work, you got to treat them bad. You treat them like people, they're soon going to believe they are as good as you and me. You are a fool," the other voice said.

"I respectfully disagree with you," said the voice named Edward, his speech strange to Bright's ears. "My family and I will treat our slaves like human beings. If we are to save them from the pagan religions of their past, we must do so."

"That's why you are not making any money on that poor stand of cotton at Raveneau this year," said the other man. "Old man Raveneau would roll over in his grave, given he knew how soft you have become on his slaves. He would be sorely sorry that he let you marry his little girl if he knew you let that place go to rack and ruin after he be gone."

"Ah, I think I have found the man I'm seeking! Over here, Charles." The man's voice sounded suddenly relieved. Then he added, "And I will beg to take your leave, sir."

"Mark my word, you'll live to rue the day you treat slaves like human beings," the second man added, his voice growing faint.

Bright heard Papa's booming voice approaching. "Why, Edward Haverford, what a sight for sore eyes you be!"

"Charles Cameron, as I live and breathe. I heard from a drover who camped near you that you would arrive today," said the man who had been waiting. "How are things up on your mountaintop? Still as cold and damp as it was when last I sat at your table?"

"It be a mite cooler even in my forge than down here in this clachan. This place feels like the devil's own boiling pot, it does," said Papa affably.

"Do you ever hear news of Big Tom?" asked Mr. Haverford. "Did they sell him downriver? Or did he run away to Canada, as I have heard from some of my slaves?"

"I heard a rumor from a traveler to my forge that Big Tom made it safely to Canada and that he has a fine life there," said Papa, speaking quickly. Then he added, "Do you remember Andrew? And Bright is around here somewhere."

Papa walked around to the front of the wagon as Bright rushed to stand, brushing the grass and dust from her skirts and apron.

The stranger was shaking hands with Andrew as they walked toward her. She curtsied as Ma had taught her, and Mr. Haverford laughed in delight as he came forward and kissed her cheek, one hand hidden in his pocket even on so hot a day.

"She's growing to be a great beauty, Charles, albeit she looks much like you!" said Edward, laughing as Bright's face turned scarlet. "Miss Bright, I hope for you to meet my little daughter, Daphne. I think you two will get on famously."

Turning to face Papa, he added, "When can you come to sup with us? We are at the town house this week for the parties during the fall sales. I want to talk to you about finishing off a smith's apprentice. He is good, but you could show him the finer points. I've never known a finer smith."

"After the sale is finished this morning," said Papa. "Would noonday dinner be acceptable? We will talk about the apprentice, then we can be on our way home early this sundown."

Mr. Haverford frowned slightly. "We eat our big meal at noon on the farm, but in town all the ladies serve their formal meal at night. Can you not stay another day? Please."

The man looked like Andrew when he pleaded for a second slice of pie, Bright thought.

Papa considered the suggestion for a moment, then he shook his head. "I have left Mairi alone on that mountaintop long enough. We must leave the city later today."

"Then I will see if Cook can fix a light repast before your departure. I am sure Lily can arrange it," said Edward. "I will send my man, Caesar, around noon. He will come to carry you over in the carriage. Until then, good day, Charles. Bright. Andrew."

As he tipped his hat to Papa, Mr. Haverford pulled his hand out of his pocket. Bright could see huge jagged scars that made his hand look like an animal's claw, drawn inward with the fingers curved in grotesque arcs. It was the same hand on which Papa was branded.

Bright had held her breath, staying very quiet during the entire conversation, but as soon as the man was out of earshot, her voice burst into the words she had been thinking. "Papa, he owns slaves! I heard him talking."

"Yes, I know he does," said Papa. "He was indentured with me. After Marcus helped us escape, he took the identity of a nobleman in England, a man who died with no male heir, so his secret is safe. He and I have often spoken of his situation. He sees a conflict between his past in servitude and his ownership of slaves, but he has not yet found the will to solve that conflict. He gained a large plantation, a genteel life, and a great number of slaves in his marriage. He knows that I do not hold with slavery. I know he owns slaves. We were friends before these things were true."

Bright could hardly believe that Papa would be friends with a man who owned slaves while he risked his own life to help them escape from their owners. "Papa, how can you?" she asked sternly.

"A man lives in a world not of his own making, my Brightie," said Papa. "I cannot control another man's beliefs. This nation is a free nation for a man to believe whatever he wishes. I may not agree, but what he does I cannot control."

"Except for the slaves. They cannot believe whatever they want. They cannot even be free!" said Bright, her voice raised in anger. "And he was once a slave himself. How could he?"

"Bright, hush," said Papa softly, so softly she had to listen carefully. "We are not on the mountain now. We are in the midst of land where slavery is a way of life. We must keep our thoughts to ourselves and go about our business with courtesy and refinement. To do otherwise might endanger us. I know you can do that, my Brightie."

"Are we going to Edward Haverford's house for noonday dinner, even though he owns slaves?" asked Bright. "How can we?"

"We are going to visit the home of an old friend, whether we believe in his way of life or not," said Papa. "Andrew, prepare yourself for the morning's sale. Bright, you will go with me to Haverford's while Andrew guards the wagon for us."

CHAPTER 13 ∂⟋

LATER THAT MORNING a tall man, his skin as black as a raven's wing, helped Bright climb into a high carriage to sit opposite Papa on a velvet cushion so soft that she could not stop touching it with her fingertips.

As they rode through tree-lined streets, Papa began to sing a song she had often heard him sing on the mountain.

> *"I will sing again of a place called home,*
> *A place where bright freedom's song can ring with the bells*
> *and sing through the skies,*
> *a place of bright freedom, a place of all glory, a place of*
> *bright freedom's song."*

When he had finished, Papa began to sing his song again. As they turned the corner to travel a long driveway lined with trees, Bright realized that the coachman was singing very softly. She hummed until Papa lifted his finger to his lips indicating that she should be silent.

Bright was puzzled, but the house at the end of the driveway soon made her forget her confusion.

The coach stopped. As the coachman swung the steps down for them to alight, the door of the house flew open, and a young girl came skipping down the pathway, followed by a Negro girl about the same height.

"I am Daphne Haverford," the girl said with a curtsy. "My papa is waiting for you, Mr. Cameron. You must be Bright. Oh, I am so happy you came to sup with us!"

Daphne talked so fast that she made Bright's head spin, but hers was such a happy voice that it was impossible not to feel happy with her.

As Daphne took Bright's hand, she said, "Let's go see my playhouse while our papas are talking. Come with me."

Skipping around the corner of the house, Daphne was careful to stay on the stepping-stones in the path, her blond curls bouncing with every step, leaving Bright to make her way through mud and pine straw strewn beside the walkway. The other girl followed the pair, walking primly and carefully on the stepping-stones.

Finally Daphne dropped Bright's hand as she ran to stand facing her on a tiny porch of a house that looked like a miniature of the big house. The brown-skinned girl disappeared through the door of the miniature house, her hoops swaying as she walked.

Although Bright had seen ladies in their carriages on the turnpike wearing hoops, she had had no idea that girls her age wore them. They would, she thought, make it very difficult to run and herd sheep.

"Come on in," Daphne said, bending to enter the tiny house. Daphne talked on, not waiting for an answer as she stuck her head through the small window to see if

Bright was following. "Cook will send Cain out with some dinner for us. We are invited to join the adults for tarts afterwards. Do you like pudding tarts, Bright? Cook is making them this day. She let me lick the stirring spoon just as you arrived. Oh, I love pudding tarts!"

Bright lowered her head to walk into the tiny house. A small table was set with a white cloth and silver cutlery. Small dishes painted with flowers sat at every place, marked by a napkin in a silver holder. A tiny teapot covered by a cozy sat on a side table. The brown-skinned girl stood silently behind the teapot, her hands folded in front of her, smiling slightly. She still had not spoken.

Daphne went on, "Mamá says that, as a special treat because you are our guest, Cain may bring us some real English tea with lemon and sugar to have with lunch. Won't that be so good? We are having hot scones with jam and cream. Ours is so much better than the adults are having. Oh, I am so happy that you came!"

Bright felt as if she were drowning in a river of words as Daphne spoke. She looked around, searching for something to say, and finally blurted, "What bonny dishes, miss."

"I'm not 'miss,' except to the slaves," said Daphne.

Still searching for things to say to cover her wonderment at the tiny house, Bright said, "Daphne, do you help your mother with the work in the house?"

Daphne stopped talking to look at Bright as if she were seeing her for the first time. "Work in the house? I don't do that, of course. That is the job of the house slaves. Cuba and Cain do everything for me. They play with me, so I never get lonely."

Bright wondered if Daphne realized that her playmates were owned by her papa. Or if she knew her papa had once been in bondage like they were. She wondered if any of these things troubled Daphne, but Daphne did not seem troubled at all.

Daphne examined the table and handed a spoon to Cuba, who polished it with a rag she suddenly had in her hand. Then she handed the spoon back to Daphne, who continued to talk rapidly as she placed it back on the table.

She stopped talking, looked at Bright in puzzlement, then after a moment said, "Do you do such work? Why don't you just have your slaves do those things?"

"We don't have slaves," Bright explained, trying to choose her words carefully. Papa had reminded her that, whatever her beliefs, she was a guest in Daphne's home and should speak carefully.

Then a new idea dawned on Daphne as Bright hesitated. "Is your papa too poor to have slaves? Do you do *all* the work?"

"Our papa doesn't think that having riches has anything to do with it. He chooses not to have slaves. He wants his children to be able to do anything they are faced with," Bright continued.

Daphne indicated that Bright should sit on the opposite side of the table. Cuba pulled out a chair for Daphne, then took Bright's chair from her hands, indicating that she should walk around and sit down.

CHAPTER 14 ∂⌒

A SOFT KNOCK SOUNDED at the door, and it was opened by a boy carrying a heavy silver tray. His face looked exactly like Cuba's. Bright looked from one to the other. It was like seeing two people with the same face.

"Come in, Cain," said Daphne. "This is my guest, Bright. Cuba and Cain are twins."

The boy nodded slightly as Daphne motioned for him to set the tray on a smaller table near them. He lifted a silver cover, and Cuba passed the scones. Then Bright followed Daphne's example in spreading the white napkin across her lap.

Cain went to stand beside the table with Cuba, his hands behind him. The pair was silent as Daphne laughed and talked. At the Cameron house, sweets were rarely a part of any meal. Here, a great pot of jam had been placed on the table so that she could take all she wanted. After helping herself to thick cream to spread on the scones and to strawberry jam to spread on top, Bright began to eat. She thought she had never tasted anything quite so fine.

When they had finished, Daphne turned to Cain. "You may take away our plates now, Cain. And I will pour the tea. Then we're off to the parlor to have pudding tarts with Mama and Papa. Then I will have my pianoforte lesson in the music room."

Silently, the boy cleared the table as Daphne poured tea into each cup and passed tiny slices of lemon. Daphne licked her slice of lemon, then dropped it into her tea. Bright bit into her slice. It was so sour that she frowned. Then, following Daphne's example, she dropped the lemon slice into her teacup.

Cain hurried to pass another pitcher of cream, tiny blocks of white sugar, and a silver spoon to each girl. It seemed very strange to Bright that a boy should wait on the table. As he offered the spoons, Bright asked Cain, "Do you always take care of us and pass the spoons? Or do you work with Mr. Haverford sometimes?"

"No, miss," Cain said quietly. "I belong to Miss Daphne."

Then Bright remembered that Cain was a slave. But somehow she had never thought of someone her age owning slaves!

"You belong to Daphne?" asked Bright very quietly.

"Well of course he belongs to me," said Daphne, laughing. "Papa gave him and Cuba to me so I would never be lonely. They are my playmates."

Bright did not know what to say, so she nodded slightly and took a sip of tea.

When they had finished, Daphne led Bright along the stepping-stones toward the big house, where they joined the adults until it was time for Daphne's music lesson.

Then Mrs. Haverford walked with Bright out to the veranda and invited her to sit in a big wicker chair—shaded by a vine that hung from the roof to the ground—where she could wait for Papa. Bright could hear Daphne's voice, then a few notes on the pianoforte, then the teacher's voice before the notes began all over again.

The chair was so soft, and she was so full of jam and pudding, that Bright pushed her head into the pillows. She began to plan how she would describe her visit to the Haverford house. Voices startled her, voices from two people hidden by the vine that shaded her chair.

A young girl's voice—it sounded like Daphne's slave Cuba—was saying in distress, "No. No. No."

Bright rose to her feet, ready to ask if she could help, but stopped when she heard Cain's voice saying, "But it's a chance to be free, Cuba, before Master Haverford parts us and sells one of us. We been together since we born. Our ma birthed us on the same day. We be like one person in two bodies. Please, Cuba."

"I don't care if I free or not"—Cuba's voice. "Why I want to be free? I have Miss Daphne to play with me. I have good food, pretty dresses. What else do I want?"

Cain's voice argued. "Which one of us Master going to sell? I don't want to go without you."

"Miss Daphne sic the dogs on me if I go," said Cuba. "I be her playmate. We always been friends."

"Caesar say that Master's rice crop is poorly this year," said Cain. "He may have to sell some of us to keep his land. We don't serve no good purpose, 'ceptin' to keep Miss Daphne out'n Miss Lily's hair. We may be the first to go. Please, Cuba." His voice was pleading.

"You run," said Cuba angrily, "if you want to. You

do, I never speak to you again. I tell Master you run. Where you going to run to?"

"I run," said Cain, slowly and softly. "You never see me again. I be gone for good."

"For good?" asked Cuba. "For good and forever? I never see you again?" She began to cry.

"Never again," said Cain.

Bright could hear Cuba's sobs and Cain's voice saying, "Shh. Don't cry."

Stepping back to her chair, Bright looked around. As her papa and Mr. Haverford stepped through the doorway onto the porch, she leaped up and ran to meet them. She must not allow the adults to hear the conversation behind the vine or even to know it had occurred.

"Papa," she said very loudly, hoping to warn the pair behind the vine and, at the same time, to keep the adults from hearing them. "This has been a wonderful visit. This beautiful house—and Daphne—and the scones." She made her words run together.

"I am so glad you enjoyed your visit," Mr. Haverford said. "You'll have to come down and spend a fortnight with Daphne next season."

Bright glanced at Papa. There were questions in his eyes, and she dared not answer them now. She would have an opportunity to later.

CHAPTER 15 ∞

ALL THE WAY UP the mountain, Bright talked of the wondrous visit with Daphne, the jam and scones, the tarts, the playhouse, the painted dishes, the silver teapot, and Daphne's Cain and Cuba, telling Andrew every detail she could remember.

But she was thinking, too. *How strange it must be to have your papa buy playmates for you. How strange it must be to own other people.* She could not imagine having someone her own age belong to her and wait on her. The twins seemed to be well treated but, even so, they were owned and could be sold away if Mr. Haverford's crops were poor. The day had given Bright a new view of slavery. Even when she had helped slaves near her own age when they found their way to the Cameron farm, even when Lloyd and Evie had come to the mountain, slavery had seemed far away.

This day, and the visit to the Haverford house, had made it all very real.

"Do they really *belong* to her?" asked Andrew as the wagon rocked side to side.

"As much as one person can ever belong to someone else, they do," said Papa. "Edward has given them to her to keep her company and to care for her. That was a choice he made. We need not agree with his choice."

"She also has a maid, Arty, to care for her clothes and her person. That's what she told me," said Bright. "Does she own her, too?"

"As much as one person can own another," repeated Papa. His face was worried. "I may have made an error in judgment in taking you to Edward's house."

"If owning slaves means that you can have jam and cream and tarts every day, then I want to own slaves like Mr. Haverford," said Andrew.

Bright looked at Andrew in disgust. At almost ten years, he seemed so very young and without a serious thought. There were so many things her brother did not yet understand.

"I am sure that Edward's slaves are well treated, but they are not free. They can be sold to a master who is a brute at any minute. And if things don't change soon, he will need to sell some of them if he is to keep his land," said Papa.

He sighed and shook his head as Andrew made a place for himself in the wagon bed, among the barrels of flour, the sack of sugar, and the large sack of coffee, so fragrant that it tickled Bright's nose each time she turned around.

"Don't worry, Papa," said Bright, moving to the wagon seat beside Papa. "I liked visiting Daphne's playhouse. I liked the scones and jam, too. But I like our farm on Mairi Mountain with you and Ma ever so much more." She leaned against his arm, feeling his muscles move as he guided the oxen up the steep slope where the climb to the top of the Blue Ridge Mountains began.

Soon Andrew was asleep, his head on the sugar sack. Bright could finally talk to Papa. He spoke softly to Bright, explaining what he had heard from Haverford.

"The Fugitive Slave Act has now been given stronger teeth," said Papa. "It be now more dangerous than ever for us to aid a slave in running. A man or his family could be hanged for hiding a slave. So you know our work becomes even more secret now, my daughter?"

Bright shuddered. The thought terrified her. Papa and Ma could be hanged. She might be hanged, too.

"We must do our duty to all those held in servitude as I once was. I must help this evil system to be destroyed. I must make sure that such a system never threatens my children. Nor the other friends I love, as Marcus is threatened every day he lives!"

"But Mr. Haverford owns slaves. He seems to be a good man," said Bright. "I thought that only bad men owned slaves."

"Ah, my Brightie," said Papa. "Many a good man's not able to give up his soft life. I read that the great American leader Thomas Jefferson owned many slaves. He wrote that were it not for the work of his slaves, he could not lead the life he enjoyed. Yet he did not free his slaves. He was the man who wrote that we are all created equal. If we are all equal, how could he own other men?"

"Did Mr. Haverford own slaves when you were indentured?" asked Bright.

"No, an indentured man may own nothing."

"How did he get so many slaves, then?" asked Bright.

"Edward was in love with a pretty girl on the small farm nearby, the daughter of a yeoman. Mr. Plaquemens, our master, wanted that farm and forced her father off his land. The winter was very cold, and Edward's love died from the lung disease. He swore then that his family would never again be poor."

"How did he become so rich, Papa?" Bright insisted.

"After we escaped, Edward passed himself off as English gentry. He took a knife to his branded arm and tried to erase the scars. He lost the use of his hand. He had learned manners of the gentry back in England, so people believed his story of a hunting wound," said Papa. "When he met the only daughter of Old Man Raveneau at a frolic, he courted her as if his life depended on it. I guess it did, in a way. The old man died soon after they were married, so the family never sought to learn of Edward's lineage."

"He has a fine life," said Bright. "I can see wanting a life like that."

"On the backs of other men?" said Papa sharply.

"No, Papa," she replied, her eyes stinging with tears. Her papa seldom, if ever, chastised her. Now his tone did, even if the words did not. She was silent, lost in thought for a while. Then she asked, "If one of Mr. Haverford's slaves should run away, would you help her?"

"Her?" asked Papa, glancing at Bright. "Who might be running, Brightie?"

"No one," said Bright quickly. "I only wondered if you would help a slave to run when you know that her, uh, his master is your old friend, and if you know the master needs the money the sale of that slave would bring. That would be a hard thing to decide, Papa."

"Many things are hard to decide, Brightie," said Papa, watching her carefully. "Do you think we will have to decide soon?"

"I don't know, Papa," she said. "I overheard two people talking. Cuba and Cain, the twins who belong to Daphne. They might run."

"Then we need to decide what we will do, my Brightie," said Papa.

But Papa continued, almost as if speaking to himself, "Edward's way of life may not last long. The land is too worn-out to grow cotton like it once did. There is talk of northern markets buying Egyptian cotton to protest the use of slaves to grow it here. Most Southern states have no factories. If they have no market for their cotton, their whole system will collapse. The market for rice is holding, but that may change now that Commodore Perry has opened up trade with Japan. The crops that need a system of slavery may disappear in a few years. When that happens, their way of life is gone."

"Will that hurt us?" asked Bright. "Up on our mountain?"

"Only a wee bit," said Papa. "We will have fewer wagons passing on their way to summer homes. Mayhap fewer wagons carrying goods will pass. But we are self-sufficient. We can take care of our own and a few who may pass through."

"What will happen to Mr. Haverford and his family?" said Bright.

"They will lose their money, their slaves, and their whole way of life," said Papa. "And if South Carolina leaves the union, as the talk is at the market, they may lose it much sooner. We are likely to have a rebellion against the Federal government that will not allow the states to decide if they be slave or free. Perhaps it will be an all-out war," he added, shaking his head sadly.

"A war, Papa?" said Bright. She had heard many stories about the Mexican War, when the men of the mountains had gone all the way to New Orleans to fight, and the war to win independence from England nearly one hundred years ago.

"A war, my Brightie," said Papa. "A war that will see brother fighting brother. It may destroy this nation. That will be a sad day. Ah, a sad day indeed."

After they made camp that night, Bright lay looking up at the stars. A shooting star slashed the darkness, seeming to open the sky. Papa's words about the possibility of war worried her. Bright did not exactly know what a war was. She only knew that it was a bad thing. But so was slavery.

CHAPTER 16 ⁊◌

1861

THAT WINTER BRIGHT TURNED fourteen. The snow blew until it was piled high, and the rivers froze. It was the coldest within living memory, said most folks who stopped by the forge. Ma and Bright worked hard to make sure the people in their care were fed and clothed to be sent on their way up the spine of the Blue Ridge Mountains toward freedom.

The cellar beneath the corncrib, the root cellar, and the new room under the forge each had at least one new face almost every day during the winter. Papa said that any person left out in the cold in such weather would freeze to death within a night. Women were often kept under the forge, although the place posed a greater danger of discovery, because it was warmed by the fire above, their children drugged with herbs so they would not cry out.

Bright completed all the tasks assigned to her, although her back sometimes grew tired and her arms ached from the hard work and the loads she carried. She did not mind helping prepare the food or carrying pots of stew and buckets of water to the corncrib, where stairs to the underground world were hidden beneath a trapdoor under the straw. The task she hated most was helping Andrew carry the slop jars to be emptied in the privy, then washing them in the creek and returning them to the hiding places. So Ma reminded her that even that most menial and distasteful task was an important part of keeping the hiding places clean and their travelers safe and healthy. Bright tried to remember that, each time she trudged through the snow. Helping with the work might be important, she thought, but it was sometimes very unpleasant.

One cold night, when the parson's wagon had been left overnight for repairs, Bright carried a pot of soup to the corncrib. Making sure that the trapdoor was covered with hay and straw to help keep the warmth of the earth below and keep out the cold, Bright knocked three times, left the pot, and had turned to go when she heard a voice singing softly, "Bright freedom's song, a song of freedom . . ."

The voice sounded familiar. Looking into the gathering darkness at the edge of the small building, she saw a man in the shadows. Surely, if Marcus were there, he would speak her name. Then she covered her mouth to stop her surprised gasp as she saw Mr. Haverford's coachman, Caesar. He was singing Papa's song from their ride in the carriage.

"Miss Bright," the tall man began. "I was sent to bring Mr. Edward's Toby to the neighbor's house. He will be here tomorrow to begin working in the forge."

"Papa will recognize you," Bright began, explaining the situation to herself more than to the coachman.

"I know," the man said quietly. "I ran Mr. Edward's wagon off the mountainside with my hat in it. I sent his horse into the woods. He will make his way back home, or someone will steal him. No one can trace anything to your papa. I want to make free. Will you help me? Your papa's song said ..." He faltered, not knowing what to say.

Bright quickly said, "While I go to get Papa, knock three times on the floor. Only then will someone push up the door. You will be safe there. This is a safe house."

"Where am I?" the man asked, frightened.

"You are in North Carolina, but we are not slaveholders. As far as we know, no one suspects our work," she said. "I will bring Papa."

Running through the snow, Bright called to Papa at the forge, being careful to say only that he was needed at the house.

Toby, the new apprentice, Papa had said, was to know nothing about the safe house nor the hiding places for runaways. Papa had made it clear that Toby was an apprentice, not an indentured servant, and that he was not to be trusted with their secret. One hint of the work might cost any of them their lives. Bright was careful never to speak to Toby alone.

Papa explained that it had been necessary to take the boy. He needed help at the forge, and to refuse would arouse suspicion. Bright knew that she would have to be very careful while Toby was her papa's helper. But he must not find out. He must not.

CHAPTER 17 ∂⊙

PAPA WAS PLEASED with Toby's work. At fourteen years, the boy proved to be a fast learner and a steady worker. Although he took his noonday dinner with the family, he ate his other meals at the home of the neighbors, where Papa paid a small stipend for his board and keep. Papa worked him hard, but he talked to the boy as if he were a man.

Papa had decided that it was time, too, for Andrew to learn the skills of a smith. He placed Andrew in Toby's charge, with a stern command that the young man make a smith out of his son. Andrew resented the older boy's authority, so they could be heard in constant arguments at the forge or whenever Papa sent them to round up the sheep and move them to new pasture. Finally Bright realized that Toby's conflict with Andrew kept the apprentice too involved to notice certain activities around the Cameron household and the forge.

Toby never complained about the work of the forge, but he did not like his occasional role as a shepherd. He vowed that he had come to learn the trade of a smithy, and that shepherding had not been a part of the agreement. He protested, but his duties did not stop. Bright noticed that when an important shipment of bundles was to be picked up, Papa always sent Toby away, with an excuse to move the sheep or to cut wood for the forge fire.

One day early in the spring, Mr. Haverford came to check on Toby's progress and to ask if the neighbors had brought word of his wagon and his slave, both of which seemed to have disappeared. Bright listened as she sat close to the fire of the forge in an attempt to throw off the wind's chill as she went over Papa's accounts. Toby kept asking her to move her feet away from the fire as he circled the table that held the anvil, where he shaped horseshoes. Each time she shrugged, moved, and then turned back to the fire.

Bright almost missed what Papa was saying, but she heard, "Losing a man's property is a hard lot, my friend, as you and I well remember. But, as you also remember, losing a man's freedom is also a hard lot."

"I don't understand," said Mr. Haverford, cradling his grotesque hand in his good one, as if hiding his branded scar. "I liked Caesar. I do not understand why he would want to leave me. He was not restless, not uncontented with his lot, which was an easy one. Food, a warm room, easy work. I treat my slaves well, for I remember what it is to be hungry. And cold."

Mr. Haverford shivered, and Papa said quickly, "Brightie, lift the pewter mugs down from the rafters. Let us heat a dram of cider. Edward needs something to take off the chill."

Bright poured the cider carefully from the jug Papa

kept in the storage room. Then she lifted one of the pokers, orange-hot from the fire, and stuck its point into a cup of cider, holding it there until the liquid bubbled. Then she handed the cup to Mr. Haverford, placed the poker back into the fire, and lifted another to heat her father's cider.

When she had heated a cup for herself, she returned to sit on her stool while Toby and Andrew heated cups for themselves.

"Of your kindness to your slaves, I have no doubt," said Papa, sipping slowly, the steam rising from his cup, which he had shaped at his own forge. "For you do remember, as I do, what it is like."

"I think someone killed Caesar and took the wagon," said Mr. Haverford, drinking the cider in one long gulp. "I don't think he would run, do you?"

"A man never knows what is in another man's heart," said Papa. "For only God can read what may be writ there."

"Then you think that slaves are human, too?" asked Edward. "That they have souls?"

"I think that all men have human souls," said Papa, agreeing. "And I think slaves are human."

"But so many are running these days!" Mr. Haverford shook his head in wonderment. "The price of cotton is falling. The mills up north are buying cotton from overseas. If things don't change, I will have to sell the house in town and live on the farm full-time."

"Sounds like hard times," agreed Papa, nodding his head.

"And now that that blackguard Lincoln, with his abolitionist talk, has been elected, by however narrow a margin, and my home state has seceded, I don't know what this world is coming to." And Mr. Haverford shook his head in dismay at recent turns of events. Then he brightened. "At least if we go to war, the price of cotton will go up, and a war may save the South."

"Sell, and move up here into God's country," said Papa, indicating the sweep of the far horizon where the edge of the Blue Ridge gave way to the valley far below. "There be no talk of war here."

"It is too cold for me," said Mr. Haverford. "And you must work too hard to live. Why, you do not even have a slave for the heavy work of the forge. No, this life, my friend, is for you, mayhap, but not for me."

Rising to walk to his carriage, Mr. Haverford said, "So you think you can turn Toby into a smith by the time his apprenticeship is up?"

Papa grinned and slapped his friend on the shoulders.

"He will be a fine smithy, one with spirit and drive. He be filled with new ideas—not all of them worthy, but new ideas just the same," said Papa. "I will send him down later in the spring to you ready to open his own forge and make a fine living for you as a smith."

Finally Mr. Haverford said bitterly, "Nor would I extend his service, whatever happens to me. I well remember the despair of that situation for you. But let me hear if you get word of Caesar or my wagon, will you?"

"I will send word, if any comes this way," said Papa as Edward climbed into the carriage, assisted by a new slave in a long coat and stovepipe, looking like the newspaper photographs of President Lincoln.

Bright watched as the phaeton rolled down the road and disappeared.

"How did you keep from telling him without lying?" she asked, placing her arm around her papa's waist.

"I never lie," said Papa. "Most folks be listening for what they want to hear, not for what is said. But I am still torn between loyalty to my friend and what he considers to be his property, and my loyalty to an ideal that all men be free. I don't yet have an answer to that dilemma."

"I am proud of you," Bright whispered, feeling sure that Papa would always do the right thing, always take what he believed to be the best path to follow. She hoped she would always have such courage.

CHAPTER 18 ☙

AFTER MR. HAVERFORD LEFT, Toby fell into a strange mood. Only a few months older than Bright, he thought he knew much about the world outside the mountain farm. Sometimes Bright was irritated by his attitudes. He boasted endlessly about the fine life he was planning to lead in the city when his indentureship was up, when he had his own forge. He often boasted to Andrew that he would buy slaves to work in his forge so that he would not have to work as hard as Charles Cameron did. And he would own no sheep, so he vowed.

After one noonday dinner, Andrew, goaded beyond endurance, hit the older boy with his fists at those words against his father. But he was no match for the larger, older Toby, his arms developing from days at the anvil. Toby picked Andrew up and threw him to the ground. Andrew struggled to his feet, both fists ready to hit the older boy again.

Papa came running from the house, where he had

stayed after the meal to have a cup of coffee with Ma, and pulled the boys apart.

"I will have no fighting on my place," said Papa harshly. "You live in peace here, no matter what your disagreements be!"

"He keeps telling me about all the slaves he is going to buy when he is a smithy," said Andrew. "And he knows we don't hold with slavery here."

"We may not hold with slavery," said Papa, "but a man has a right to his opinions and his dreams as well, my Andrew. So leave him to his own words. You need not agree with them."

After sending Andrew off to the high pasture to check on the sheep, Papa sat beside Toby on the bench outside the door of the forge and spoke seriously to him.

"Young man," said Papa, "you will be a fine smith one day. You have the hands, the mind, the way of seeing things before they are fully formed. You will likely be a rich smith, a man of influence. But you would do well to look to your own work, not that of slaves. For it may be that by the time you are a smith, no slaves will be there to work for you."

"No slaves?" said Toby. "People have always had slaves. Don't you remember that Joseph and the Children of Israel were slaves of the Egyptian pharaohs? I plan to own a great many slaves. And have a fine wife of great beauty."

With those words, he looked up at the porch, where Bright was shaking the tablecloth to rid it of crumbs. She could not hear what Toby was saying to Papa, but she was startled to see Papa's jaw drop in surprise as Toby walked away, smiling broadly up at her. She was startled by Toby, who rarely noticed her, but even more startled by her father's expression. Never had she seen her father so shocked he could not speak.

Bright went back into the kitchen, thinking of Toby's smile. He hardly looked at her during meals, and he never spoke except to mumble his gratitude as she passed a platter across the table at his request. She often wished she could talk with him, but his silence when she was around made it much easier to keep her family's work a secret.

Toby avoided her as usual until one evening when spring had arrived, then departed again, leaving the streams frozen and the early flowers burnt brown. A dusting of snow covering the mountain gave it a look of winter. Bright, carrying water through the snow, trying to maintain her footing on the hard ice, snow now frozen solid, did not see him as he walked up behind her. As she plunged forward, certain to land on her nose, she felt a strong arm catch her and break her fall.

Bright stared into Toby's brown eyes. Before she realized what was happening, his face touched hers, cold and chapped. Frightened, she pushed him away.

"When the war is over, I'll come back," he said. "And—"

"War?" Bright was stunned. "The war? You said, 'the war'?" she repeated.

"War," said Toby, moving away and jumping into the air, waving both arms. "We fired on Fort Sumter a few days ago!"

"War?" she said again, picking up the bucket. She had so many things to sort out. "No. No."

Toby followed her back to the stream.

"What is this war?" she asked, moving away from him, keeping her distance.

"There are Federal troops on our soil," he said. "South Carolina seceded last December. You heard me talking to Charles at noonday dinner all winter. Then Lincoln said he would keep Federal possessions in the South. Last month he sent supplies to Fort Sumter. You read all about that in the newspaper."

"But we are in North Carolina," said Bright, puzzled.

"I come from South Carolina. I was apprenticed to Haverford there," he said. "And word come up the mountain today that North Carolina will join the War for Southern Independence any day now. As soon as my apprenticeship is finished, I am joining the army."

"What army?" asked Bright.

"The army of the Confederation, of course," he said, perplexed that she would ask. "You know all that from Charles's newspapers, Bright. I will fight for the right of each sovereign state to decide its fate."

Trying to sort through all the ways her world had suddenly changed, Bright allowed Toby to carry the pail. As they walked, her mind was racing. Finally she could breathe again. She said, "Please, Toby, don't tell Papa yet. I must think on this. Please, not yet. Please."

"He already knows, Bright," said Toby. "He's known ever since South Carolina's secession that war was likely."

"No, I mean about . . ." She paused. "About what you said . . ."

Just then, as they neared the house, Papa opened the door, his face red with rage.

"Away! Away with you, Toby!" Papa shouted, grabbing the collar of Toby's heavy sweater, knocking his cap into the snow. "You will leave Brightie alone. Do you hear? Now, away with you! You are ready to join the army this day. Your apprenticeship is finished. Do not come back to the forge until I have decided what will become of you."

The following morning, long before sunup, Papa went to bring Toby from the neighbor's house and put him on the first wagon headed east.

CHAPTER 19 ෨

WITH TOBY GONE for weeks now, Andrew had become his father's sole helper at the forge. The neighbor's hired hand had gone to join the Union army. The farrier had left for a homestead in Missouri territory. Papa had been unable to find another helper. Most of the young men who passed on the turnpike were leaving to join one army or the other.

Each day a greater number of wagons, carriages, stages, and riders passed, stopping at the forge for repairs. Bright's father and Andrew worked long hours at the forge, leaving the care of the sheep and part of the work on the farm and with the runaways to Bright and her mother. As the weather grew warmer, the number of runaways increased daily, or so it seemed. Ma's bountiful garden and the animals traded to Papa in exchange for his services provided enough food, but she often spoke of her worry about the amount of food available to preserve for winter and the lack of time to preserve it.

Bright spent part of her time delivering food, making sure that the tired travelers were fed and rested when the men disappeared into the woods bordering the farm. She helped to make sure the women and children were hidden in the false-bottomed wagons Papa or other guides drove away, carrying their bundles to the next stop at another safe house several miles away. The rest of her time was spent in taking care of farm tasks and feeding the animals, leaving Papa and Andrew to run the forge.

Later, in the summer, the runaway slaves were joined by white men from the neighboring counties seeking safe passage to join the Federal armies. Bright sometimes felt that the farm was filled to bursting with people, all of them secret and hidden. The local men usually made their way through the forest with the male slaves as Papa hauled those less fit for travel on foot hidden in his wagon. But before they began their journey, he insisted that every person be fed and rested.

Ma was busy cooking stew and baking bread. Bright never seemed to finish the work she had to do. At first each person had seemed to be an individual to Bright. She had taken time to get to know each face and hear each story, but as more and more slaves seeking freedom made their way to Mairi Mountain, their faces became a blur to Bright. She wanted very much to help, but sometimes she became tired and short-tempered. Sometimes at night she felt very old and tired.

Time and again, she had asked Papa if she could help with the real work of helping the slaves make their way to freedom, driving the wagon to the next safe house. But each time, Papa said, "This is dangerous work, even for a strong man. It is not work in which my daughter will risk her life any more than she risks it here each day."

And he refused to discuss the issue. He worked all day and often traveled all night, returning to the forge as the sun rose. His skin grew pale, and dark circles formed around his eyes. His face became more gray and haggard each day.

Bright so wished there was something more she could do, but the one thing that would take the greatest burden from Papa was the one job he would never trust to her. But she knew that she could do it, if only he would give her a chance.

One evening when she was so tired that her shoulders felt as if she were carrying one of Papa's anvils in each arm, not the heavy pot of turnip greens and corn bread for the runaways, Bright turned back as she stood in the kitchen doorway.

"Ma," she said, almost sobbing, "why is it that you and I must always see to the cooking and cleaning while Papa does the really important things? I am tired of peeling potatoes, washing greens, and emptying slop jars! Why can't we do important things, too?"

Ma stopped kneading the mountain of white dough almost covering the kitchen table. She looked up and wiped her forehead on her arm, streaking her face with flour.

"Oh, Brightie, my dearest," said Ma, her expression filled with worry. "You are so tired. We all are. But we must remind ourselves that even the most menial task of peeling potatoes so those in our care may eat is just as important as the more exciting work of transporting them. The value of our lives lies in the small details that see to the well-being of those in our care. Can you remember that, my daughter?"

Bright nodded and turned her head away so Ma would not see the tears of exhaustion that slipped down her cheeks.

"I will remember, Ma," said Bright, closing the door behind her. "I will try to remember. But right now, I am so very tired," she told herself softly.

Once, late at night, Bright heard Papa telling Ma, "The danger be far too great. We cannot place our Bright in such danger. Things grow more perilous in our work each day. To put her on the road with a load is placing her in the path of harm. The pattyrollers become ever more vigilant as more slaves run. A young woman driving a wagonload of runaway slaves is in greater danger than death. Ever since North Carolina left the Union, the laws have grown more stringent and the pattyrollers more vigilant. Even their dogs are trained to kill. They starve them so they will be mean and hungry."

The Mennonite parson's wagon came for repairs less and less often, Bright noticed. She heard Papa tell Ma that the parson's house was being watched. So far the Cameron forge and farm had escaped suspicion, but that might not continue.

But when she mentioned her worries to Ma, her only reply was "Your papa has to do what he believes is right."

As the weather grew colder and the war went on, their work became more and more tiring. Through the following winter, food to feed the runaways would have been scarce if bags of potatoes, stacks of cabbages, or bunches of collards had not been placed on the porch of the Cameron house, left without a word by neighbors and passing travelers. Occasionally Bright opened the door to find a side of venison or beef hanging from a hook attached to the rafters of the front porch. Neighbors were quietly helping to make sure the work continued.

CHAPTER 20 ☙

1862

ONE DAY, WHEN THE WINTER was almost past, Papa came to noonday dinner with an air of great excitement, his face suffused with more color than Bright had seen since the summer began. Morgan the tinker had stopped that morning. Always a welcome sight at the widely scattered mountain farms, he had brought special news that day.

"Mr. Coffin, a Quaker merchant from Ohio, has been on a buying trip through the South to New Orleans, and is making his way home. He will be passing on the Buncombe Turnpike within the week," Morgan had told Papa. "He wants to stop at your forge."

Many merchants had come by the forge, and Papa met all of them. Bright wondered what was so special about Mr. Coffin.

When she asked, Ma had replied, "Why, Mr. Coffin is a worker in this endeavor we are engaged in to help the slaves to be free. He is a much respected merchant in both North and South. His home and store act as a depot for the runaways on their journey into Canada and freedom. He is one of the most important men in the movement. We must make him welcome."

Ma began such a flurry of cleaning that Bright realized how much the visit of Mr. Coffin meant to her ma as well as to her papa. The floors were scrubbed. The bedding was washed. The braided rugs were beaten. It was too early for garden vegetables to come in, and feeding so many through the winter had left the root cellar almost bare, so Ma found it hard to make a fine dinner for Mr. Coffin. A goose was penned and fed corn to fatten it for the dinner table, and good stew was made from the family's meager supply of potatoes, onions, carrots, and herbs.

Bright and Peigein scoured the meadow for the first of the greens, shoots showing near the water's edge, which Ma wilted with bacon drippings. Then she added the few spring onions growing in a corner of the garden protected from the wind. With some newly ground cornmeal baked into brown bannocks, the meal filled the house with its fragrances as Mr. Coffin's carriage arrived.

The family sat around the table while Mr. Coffin returned thanks to God for the meal they would enjoy, and Ma passed the bowls and platters, first to their guest and then to the family.

"I have heard much of your work here, Cameron," said Mr. Coffin as he buttered his second bannock and placed a crust of it in his mouth. "And you have managed to provide safety for so many without raising suspicion. That is quite remarkable."

"Much support is to be found in these hills," said Papa. "As you know, a runaway is able to follow a trail of safe houses along the spine of these mountains to the free states and the borders of Canada."

"Yes," said Mr. Coffin. "This is the major overland escape route, along with the Mississippi River and the Atlantic seaboard. Why are mountain people so involved?"

"The mountain people be a most independent lot," said Papa, taking Ma's hand in his. "They treasure their freedom beyond anything else, and they find it hard to ken why one man should own another. It sticks in their craw, as they say. Too, some of their grandsires made it across the water as I did. My good wife's grandsire and her father, for two."

Mama poured more coffee into each man's cup, then she said, "My father spent his early years in the fields serving a master—a kindly master, but a master nonetheless."

"More citizens in this country than a man would ever guess came across the waters in servitude or found themselves in bondage when they landed. Many today are a generation or two removed from it, and so they prefer to disremember it. It seems that the mountain residents hold on to their pasts more than some I've met," said Mr. Coffin.

"Truly spoken," agreed Papa. "Time moves more slowly up here. The past is more with us."

"I would have thought that having their land in the low country taken from them in times past and being forced into the mountains might have something to do with antislavery feelings here. Mountaineers might find this war a just retribution for earlier wrongs," suggested Mr. Coffin.

"That, too," said Papa, grinning. "Mountain men have long memories."

"So I've heard," said Mr. Coffin. "And your work at

this forge has meant so many have made their way to freedom. You will be long remembered by those who pass."

Papa beamed as Ma took his hand in hers. "We have had Marcus to help us. He could have a fine life, a safe life with his family in Canada. He has educated himself and has a farm. Yet he returns again and again. Both Marcus and I know what servitude is like, for we were once in servitude to the same cruel master. We wear the same brand."

Papa lifted his branded arm, so Bright thought, in defiance.

"That I have heard," said Mr. Coffin. "All the more reason for you to be involved in this work. Your safe house here at the eastern edge of the Blue Ridge is a critical point in the journey north for so many. There are several safe houses in this area, or so I've been told."

"More than might be thought," said Papa. "In the lowlands, other slaves and yeoman farmers help the run-aways with food to make it to our door. When they leave, many a mountain family provides shelter and food for any who pass, whatever their color. If a person be hungry, they will feed him. Many of them think of it only as helping out a fellow human being. They do not see themselves as part of our work, albeit they are im-portant to it. Many wish to remain apart from the strife. They have no fault with anybody. Yet they help all who make their way to their doors."

"Mountaineers are known for their grace and gen-erosity," said Mr. Coffin. "I am a Carolinian by birth, you know. Left the state because of slavery. My son still lives here, however, down in the Piedmont, where he is en-gaged in our work this day."

"So word has come to us," said Papa, nodding in acknowledgment. "The price and the keep of a slave be far too high for most yeomen farmers here or in the flatlands. That be reason enough for many to refrain from supporting the cause of the South in this war. And some fight for the right to decide about owning slaves, not to support a system they are not a part of. It will come to pass that these mountains will be filled with men who see any role they play as a futile one, or so I vow. These hills are riven with caves for a man to hide himself, from either side."

"Yes," said Mr. Coffin. "I, too, believe that will come to pass. Only a small number of Southerners own most of the slaves here. But that small number of men wields enormous power in the politics of the Southern states. That small number creates the problems for those of us like you and me who would free our fellow man."

Bright watched proudly as Papa nodded in agreement. "We be so far removed from the capital that it is sometimes weeks before we hear news of what takes place in the legislature. Most times the laws do not affect us, so we pay little mind to them. I am much concerned, however, with how the slaves will fare if they be freed. They have no land, no way to live save to work for their masters. I fear they will look back to slavery as a time of plentiful food and shelter, albeit without freedom to control their own lives."

"Ah, Cameron," replied Mr. Coffin. "You are a man who thinks ahead. I like that. I have it on good authority that as soon as President Lincoln can bring the rebellious states back into the Union, plans are under way to solve such problems. We would do well to look to our neighbor to the north, where some of the problems have already been addressed. In Canada, the first order of business for freed slaves has been education and jobs. I assume that will be the first order of business once the slaves are freed here as well."

"After food and shelter," said Papa. Bright was surprised to hear her father speak curtly to their honored guest. "It is a hard thing to preach freedom to a man whose stomach is growling from hunger and whose children are crying from cold."

"You are right, Cameron," agreed Mr. Coffin. "The body must be cared for before the soul can be fed." He paused.

"And we fed so many, we would have run out of food but for the gifts left at our door last winter," said Bright.

"Those of our neighbors who had plenty shared with our family," said Ma. "We depend on one another here as if we were family."

"And in a way, those of us who help other humans are like a family. It is good of your neighbors," said Mr. Coffin. "Say, Cameron. Do you know what our work in transporting men to freedom has come to be called in Ohio?"

"We get not much news of Ohio down here, save from guides who pass through to lead the fugitives," said Papa, eager to hear how their work was thought of in the country where the slaves were headed.

"We are recently called the Underground Railroad," said Mr. Coffin. "The abolitionist newspapers call our efforts by that name because the runaways disappear here in the South and are seen again only in free states or in Canada."

"The Underground Railroad," mused Papa. "It is neither underground nor is it a railroad. But mayhap the name suits it."

"It is far less organized than an outsider would assume," said Mr. Coffin. "It seems that people who want to help simply appear, do their work, then disappear. And it is my belief that certain abolitionists take more credit than is deserved for the movement of slaves. In my experience, slaves who cannot or will not escape down here are most valuable in helping others with a chance of success."

"Let us not forget the ones like Marcus, who risk not only their freedom, so hard gained," said Papa. "Many of us owe him our lives."

"True. True," agreed Mr. Coffin. "The Negroes, slave, former slaves, and free men and women, they take the greatest risks and do the most important work. The rest of us only provide support. And after that fine meal, Mrs. Cameron, I fear I must take my leave..."

But his words were cut off by the sound of hoofbeats as a rider threw himself to the house porch and pushed open the door. Morgan the tinker stood in the doorway, his cap in his hands.

"They's troops riding up the turnpike, Southern troops," he said. "I thought to warn you, Mr. Coffin. Ellis, the guide, is waiting at the ford of the Hungry River to see you safely out of the area."

"I have long traded down here," Mr. Coffin said, rising from his chair and shaking hands with Papa. "But I'll take my leave now. With the blockade of Charleston Harbor, it won't be long before traders with goods to sell will be a welcome sight. Before my return, would you and Mrs. Cameron come to Ohio for a visit, perchance?"

"I must put my affairs in order here. Mayhap when

the war is over," said Papa, rising to shake Mr. Coffin's hand. "Much obliged we be for all your work. God go with you, my friend."

As the Camerons and their guest made their way to the porch, the tinker leaped onto his horse and galloped down the market road.

"And what was it the tinker said about a guide at the ford?" asked Mr. Coffin.

Papa started toward the barn. "I will load the wagon and carry you there."

CHAPTER 21 ✍

NEWS OF THE VICTORIES and defeats of Federal troops and Southern regiments reached Mairi Mountain daily, brought by farmers returning from the market with their pockets filled with bills, issued by the treasury of the Confederation of Southern States and earned from the highest prices their livestock had ever brought.

As Papa had predicted, his work at the forge increased. In summer, planters brought their families up the mountain to their summer homes to escape the heat and the problems of the towns. City residents moved to the country for the duration of the war. More mountain people than ever seemed to travel to the flatlands. Horses, oxen, and wagons passing on the market road meant more work for the Charles Cameron forge.

Each week, the number of slaves, especially young men, who stopped at the forge increased. Most of them had chosen their masters' absences as a time to escape. Many of them planned to travel with men from Henderson and Polk counties to join the Federalists from

Madison, Yancey, and Mitchell counties on their way to the Union forces mustering in Tennessee and Kentucky.

Papa worked day and night. His face grew yellow and sickly. His hair seemed to thin. As the heat of summer grew stronger, Bright heard him coughing every evening, and sometimes he moaned from pain in his chest. Still he went to the forge every day. Each week, more and more of the work of the forge was shifted to Andrew's shoulders, a heavy duty for a boy.

Finally one foggy, wet day, Papa was not able to get out of bed. Sweating profusely, he tried again and again to stand, but despite help from Bright and Ma, he fell back onto the bed. Ma wrapped him in blankets. She placed a hot poultice on Papa's chest and tucked the blankets around his chin, pinning his arms, weak from fever, so that he would not pull the flannel away.

Ma sent Peigein out to gather wild licorice roots so that she could make an infusion to clear Papa's lungs. In the meantime Bright rode down the hill on one of the horses to get some pennyroyal from Old Hannay, the herb woman. Herb tea would cause Papa to sweat and break his fever so that the licorice root could do its job more effectively.

Wishing to return quickly to help Ma, Bright jerked on the reins, urging the horse, trained to the much slower pace of the wagon and unaccustomed to being ridden, to a trot up the steep market road. As she rounded the bend in the road, she heard men's voices arguing loudly. The forge was surrounded by moving horses and an array of men dressed in a variety of brightly colored uniforms but with matching gray caps.

Bright's first thought was of the six runaways hidden in the cellar under the forge. She drew her horse to a walk and rode up to the forge, sitting as tall in the saddle as she could. If she was to protect her family's charges, she must never let the men know the fear she felt.

"Andrew, what is going on?" she called as the boy came out of the shop, his face white with fear under the black soot from the fire.

"These soldiers are having trouble with their harness. Seems that someone cut the cinches of several saddles last night," he said. "Papa is much better at harness repairs than I am. I told them he is very ill with the lung fever. They could get the harness repaired at the village upriver, but they insist that I can do it."

Bright realized that Andrew was thinking of the runaways, too. He wanted to get the soldiers on their way as soon as possible.

The man who seemed to be the leader jerked off his hat with a slight bow. "I am Lieutenant Broom, at your service, pretty lady," he said.

Bright felt her face grow scarlet, but she took a deep breath and said, with as much courage as she could muster, "Gentlemen, my father is the smith at this forge. He is very ill. My brother is only an apprentice. He is not a farrier, and he is new to leather work. You would be better served to find your way upriver, I think."

"*You* think we would be better served upriver, now do you, pretty lady?" Lieutenant Broom said, with a slight snort. "Now that I doubt." And he reached to pull her off the horse.

But she pulled her skirt away from his grasp and urged the horse up the hill.

"I must take these herbs to my papa," she said haughtily. "Surely no gentleman of the Confederacy would want to be the cause of an innocent man's death from the lung disease. Besides, what he has is catching. You may die of the same disease if you touch me. This is a dangerous place for well men to visit just now."

And she rode away toward the barn, her head high.

The uniformed men looked at one another, undecided what to do about a woman who behaved so curtly toward them. Finally Lieutenant Broom said, "Mount up, boys. We have a war to fight. And we don't need lung fever."

As the soldiers rode away, Bright dismounted and walked toward the forge. Andrew was coming to meet her. "What will we do with the bundles?" he asked.

"I don't know," she answered. "Let me think. First I need to take this pennyroyal to Ma. Has Peigein come back yet? She may be in danger. We have to find her and then get the bundles out of here. I had no thought that troops would be up this far. We have not seen any until today."

"They are scouting for runaways," said Andrew. "I heard them talking. The bundles under the forge are in danger. I think the ones in the root cellar will be safe."

"Let me think," said Bright. "I'll return when I have checked on Papa."

CHAPTER 22 🍥

MA DECIDED THAT WORK should go on at the forge as usual so that Andrew would be at the anvil if other troops came.

"I must be the one to go," said Bright. That night she might get her wish to become more involved in transporting the bundles. "There's no one else."

"Marcus will take them through the woods," said Ma. "They can walk."

"Ma, the women and their babies cannot travel fast enough to make it by morning," Bright argued. "They will be caught."

"But you can't go alone," said Ma. "You might get killed. Marcus can take the wagon."

"A Negro out at night all alone with a wagon hiding runaway slaves?" said Bright, pacing back and forth in frustration. "Ma, Marcus will be the first to be killed. I have the best chance to get them away from here. You can't leave Papa; I don't know how to care for him. Peigein is too small. Andrew needs to run the forge."

"But Bright, you are only a child," said Ma.

"I will be sixteen on my next birthday," said Bright. "It is my time to carry on the work." She paused, drew herself up so that she was taller than her mother, and repeated, "Ma, I am the only choice."

Marcus slipped into the room, and Peigein ran to greet him.

"Help me reason with her, Marcus," said Ma. "She will get you all killed."

"No, Mairi," said Marcus. He was dressed in the clothing of a farmworker, his traveling clothes. "I think young Brightie is our best chance out of here." He winked at Bright and swept his hat off in a low bow. "Why, Miss Bright, may I accompany you and your charges, ma'am?" He slurred his speech, teasing, trying to lighten the tension that hung like mist in the air of the kitchen.

"This is no time for jesting, Marcus," snapped Ma. "I understand what you are doing, but at this time..." Then she smiled up at Marcus and gave him a hug.

"This is a time for us to make the best decision," said Marcus, returning to his usual dignified posture, like that of a soldier at attention. "And that, I believe, will be for me to become Miss Bright's protector for this journey tonight. As you know, Mairi, I would lay down my life for your family. I would not intentionally endanger one of your children, any more than I would endanger my own."

"I am afraid you *will* need to lay down your life," said Ma. "Taking this child out into such danger in the middle of the night!"

"Only a little more danger than she faces here each

day," said Marcus. "Now, shall we get the papers prepared?"

Bringing Papa's wooden box, where important papers were kept, into the parlor, Ma lifted the quill pen and the ink pot and set them on the table. After mixing fresh powder and water into the ink, Bright carefully added the word *Marcus* to the blank and turned *Charles Cameron* into *Charles Cameron's daughter and representative, Bright Cameron*. She dripped some candle wax onto the paper and added a seal that, unless closely examined, looked enough like a magistrate's seal to fool all but the most expert eye.

Marcus joined hands with them around the table as they bowed their heads and asked for the blessing of a safe journey.

When they had eaten, Marcus helped lift Charles to a half-sitting position so that Mairi could spoon broth and pennyroyal tea between his weak lips.

Bright watched from the door. Her papa did not seem to know that any other person was in the room. Then Papa slept, a deep sleep broken only by a rasping sound in his chest, growing worse each time he expelled air. Bright turned away, her eyes filled with tears.

After Marcus had helped Mama wrap Papa again in quilts to make him sweat, the tall man left to help Andrew with the preparations for their journey. Peigein went to feed the chickens, while Ma opened the trunk where she kept her few pieces of fine clothing: her winter cloak, her wedding dress, and the bonnet she usually wore to church.

Slipping into Papa's room, Bright quietly sat on the floor beside his bed. Papa had managed to unwind his arms from the quilts, leaving one hand to dangle over the side. Bright took it, but she almost jumped. His hand was so hot, so feverish. She reached out to touch his face. It, too, burned to the touch. Her papa was very sick, sicker than she had realized.

Lifting his hand to her lips, she kissed the scar that marked him as once living a life of servitude, the hand that had helped so many flee their bondage as he had once flown from his to this high mountaintop. How she wished she could have erased that scar, and the pain of her father's life that the scar represented. She had to do whatever she could to help him carry on the work that had defined his life.

Bright looked at her papa, once so strong, so able to keep her safe—even from devils in the henhouse on that long ago day—and she smiled, remembering how Papa had taken his hammer to chase that "deevil" away and to calm her fears. That devil had turned out to be Marcus, the man who had saved her papa's life. Now as she looked at her papa, he seemed so frail. A new thought occurred to her: Papa might not always be there to protect her.

"Oh, Papa," she whispered, holding his hand to her cheek. "I am so sorry you are ill. I will carry on your work until you are well. I love you, Papa."

Did his hand move ever so slightly, squeezing hers so lightly that it seemed she had imagined it? She held his hand and told him of tonight's journey, of her fears, and of how she felt now that it was her duty to carry on his work. As she spoke, her heart felt lighter than it had in months, and she felt her courage returning.

Finally she stood and, placing his hand on top of the

quilt, said, "Papa, I will return safely, and I will carry on your work."

When she turned, Ma was standing in the doorway smiling slightly.

"He is very sick," said Bright.

"Yes, if his fever does not break soon . . ." Ma's voice trailed off. Shaking her head sadly, she handed Bright her old cape and helped Bright tie the ribbons of the Sunday bonnet under her chin. As she pushed her daughter's curls under the bonnet, she whispered softly, "I love you, Bright. I am so proud of you."

"I love you, too, Ma," Bright replied. "Keep my papa safe. Please."

"Please keep my daughter safe," whispered Ma.

CHAPTER 23 🌊

JUST BEFORE DARK Andrew brought the parson's wagon to the repair platform at the forge and worked on the wagon bed until three women and one baby were safely hidden under the wagon's floor, the boards not more than an inch from their noses. As the moon rose through the trees, three other figures slipped silently into the laurel thicket behind the house.

When they had finished loading the wagon with stones, Marcus checked the harness and secured the single-tree, ran his hands along the rims of the wheels, and checked to make sure the brake block was tight. Then he waited.

Mairi stepped out onto the porch, calling, "Andrew. Marcus. Hold up long enough to help me lift Charles and change his bed again. His fever has broken, and the damp bed will give him a chill."

As the two men ran to the house, Bright was coming down the steps, wearing her mother's dress and apron, a soft purple cape, and a black bonnet an older woman might wear. She had taken Papa's best rifle from its place over the door and carried it over one arm.

"You look just like your father, Bright," Ma said, her arms filled with dirty sheets. "I never realized how like him you are until today." After dropping the sheets into the black wash pot hanging from its tripod in the side yard, she hugged Bright as they walked toward the forge.

"Do not tell Papa what we have done until he is stronger," said Bright. "I don't think he heard me. Now that he is awake, he will worry so."

"Not a word to Papa," said Ma. "Don't you worry. Peigein and I will care for Papa. Andrew will see to the forge. And don't forget, Bright. You are the daughter of the smith, mature and respected, on business to deliver a load of rocks to the English farm."

"I know, Ma," said Bright peevishly. "I will remember. I know how important this journey is. I am glad that Marcus suggested the team rather than the oxen. They move so slowly."

"You must reach the English farm's safe house by daybreak, and the oxen would never make it," said Ma. "Marcus has done this many times before. He will know what to do. I am unsure about your doing this, but Marcus has always known how to take care of those he leads."

Bright turned to step on the wagon wheel but was startled to hear a night bird's cry so close to the forge that it seemed to come from a hemlock tree nearby. Marcus turned abruptly and walked to examine the tree. When he returned he said, "We have more travelers. A young boy and a young girl."

"What will we do with them? The wagon is full," said Bright. She had no energy left to think about another problem. "Take them to the house."

"I think these need go with us," said Marcus. "Now."

Bright looked startled. "Can we send them into the woods to walk near us?"

"The boy can make it, but I am not sure about the girl," whispered Marcus. "She is frail."

"Let me leave her with Ma," said Bright. "Ma can use the help."

Marcus walked slowly to the tree, then led a slender girl toward Bright. As the moon caught her pretty face and frightened eyes, Bright said before she thought, "Cuba. What are you doing here?"

Startled to hear her name, Cuba jumped. Looking at Bright, she did not seem to recognize the tall lady who stood before her. Reaching out her hand, Bright said, "Cuba, we met at Miss Daphne's little house. I know you, but you are safe here."

Cuba's head jerked in surprise. "Miss Bright?" she said.

"Yes," answered Bright. "My father is ill. I need for you to stay and help my ma until we return."

"I want to go with Cain," she said, her lip trembling. "I want to go with my brother."

"There isn't room in the wagon, Cuba," explained Bright, giving the girl's thin shoulders a hug. "I will come back and take you tomorrow. I promise."

Marcus placed his hand on the girl's shoulder. "We will take Cain to a safe place, and he can wait for you there. Mrs. Cameron needs help. Her husband is sick. If you will help her so that Bright can take Cain to safety, then I will come back for you."

"What do I have to do?" said Cuba, looking toward the tree, hoping to see Cain's face there.

"Pretend you are Mrs. Cameron's girl, helping with the sick," said Marcus. "That's all. Until tomorrow."

"All right," said Cuba. "You will come back for me? Promise?"

"We will," said Marcus as Bright took Cuba's hand and led her into the house, explaining to Ma about the twins on the way.

"You must get on your way, Bright," said Ma, settling Cuba into the kitchen. "This little lady will help me care for your papa until you return for her." Then Bright and Ma returned to the wagon.

As Marcus and Andrew helped Bright, in the unaccustomed dress and cloak, climb into the wagon, horses' hooves sounded on the road. Marcus disappeared into the shadows of the wagon platform. In the light of the lantern hanging on the brake stick, three men in blue coats rode into Bright's view. She might as well try her skills of pretending to be someone older than she was, she thought.

Lowering her voice, she said, "Good evening, gentlemen. You are on my father's property, you know. What may we do for you?"

The first soldier doffed his hat. "Ma'am, we are scouting. Looking for deserters wearing blue coats."

"Or we'll settle for gray," another man said, laughing.

Bright lifted her chin. "You'll find neither at this forge. My father lies gravely ill. We take no side in this war. Furthermore, an important delivery of stones to mend the wall at the neighbor's dam must reach that farm before it gives way and floods their crops. May we pass, please?" But her voice was not a question. It was a command.

"Yes, mistress," said the first man in blue. "Godspeed on your way."

He turned his horse toward the road, and the others followed.

"And I, too, would do what you ask in *that* tone of voice, Miss Bright," said Marcus, shaking his head in wonderment at her transformation and stepping out of the shadows. "Whew. You are *some* lady!"

"I think you will be all right," said Ma softly, smiling and shaking her head in admiration.

"Take a care, sister," said Andrew, standing beside the anvil, with more tenderness than Bright thought him capable. "Come home safe," he said, pushing back his leather hat from his forehead.

Marcus climbed up onto the seat beside her.

"You two cut a fine figure," said Ma, reaching up to take Marcus's hand. "Tearlach will be proud."

"Until we meet again, Mairi," said Marcus, tipping his hat to Ma, who blew him a kiss. "My prayers are with Charles. And with your family."

"And ours with you, Tom," said Ma. "And with my brave daughter."

"No more Tom," said Marcus. "Tom's a long time dead."

"And ours with you, Marcus," she corrected herself.

"I will take care of your daughter," said Marcus. "While she takes care of me."

Finally Marcus snapped the reins, and the wagon rolled down the road, the team moving slower than usual, confused by going on a journey into the darkness.

CHAPTER 24 ∂⌒

THE NIGHT BIRDS CALLED. The tree frogs sounded a staccato against the rush of the roaring of the water in Crooked Creek. The sounds were soothing as the wagon wheels bumped against the stones in the road, the horses guided by Marcus's steady hand on the reins.

Mourning doves called through the darkness, making a sound that always comforted Bright. Their calls were always part of the early day sounds in the woods near the house. They sounded of home. Bright's fear subsided.

As her eyes grew accustomed to the darkness, Bright realized that the moon's light allowed her to see more detail than she would have imagined. That, too, allayed her fears. She could see the turns in the road and the swath of white, splashing foam that formed first the creek and finally the river that created the valley through which the road passed. As the wagon rocked, she found her eyes closing, although she made every effort to hold them open.

She was so tired from the excitement and worry of the day. Then a deep voice spoke softly. "Bright. Bright.

We are meeting other travelers on the road. More than one horse."

Bright shook herself to clear her head. It had fallen on Marcus's arm as she fell asleep. He had not moved nor disturbed her until he heard hoofbeats ahead on the road.

Pulling the cape around her, she straightened her bonnet and pulled the cape up to hide her face until she knew who the travelers were.

The riders were making their way up the road slowly. They seemed in no hurry. Stopping their horses as the wagon approached, they waited for Marcus to bring it to a halt. In the moonlight Bright could see gray uniforms and hats like those she had seen at the forge earlier that afternoon.

A young man's voice spoke. "Who goes there?"

"My mistress and me," Marcus said, slowing his voice to a slur.

"What is your business, and you being out in the middle of the night?" the man asked. Moving his horse closer to the wagon, the man said, "And you a Negro, too? What's a black doing on the road at this hour?"

"On my massa's business," said Marcus, slurring his speech again. "We taking a load of rocks to mend a dam that's a-breaking over on the Toe River, about to flood a man's farm."

"Ain't they got no rocks on Toe River?" asked the voice.

"My massa owes a debt, and he intends to pay it afore this man's fields be gone. My massa, he got plenty rocks on his place," Marcus continued.

"And who is this with you?" the voice asked.

Bright had been quiet as long as she could stand it.

"I am the daughter of his master," she said imperiously, careful to hide her face with the cape. "We are on my father's business journey."

"And you're white!" said the voice. "A Negro out here on the road alone with a white woman. Let me see your papers."

Bright reached into her pocket and removed the document, handing it to the man and saying haughtily, "We are in a great hurry. When you are finished with the papers, we will be on our way."

The man lifted a lantern and read aloud, " 'This pass allows one Negro male, over six feet tall and more than two hundred pounds answering to the name of Marcus, to pass undisturbed in the care of one Charles Cameron's daughter and representative, Bright Cameron, on this day, July 13. Signed, Romulus Evans, Magistrate, State of North Carolina.' "

Passing the paper to another man while he examined the rocks in the wagon bed, the man said, "Your papers look to be in order. What is your destination?"

"Destination?" asked Bright. She had never heard the word before. What could it mean? She had to think quickly.

Shaking her head, she flung the hood back from the cape, leaving her face exposed as a new voice said from the shadows at the back of the group of riders, "Charles Cameron, the blacksmith on Mairi Mountain?" The voice was familiar.

"Yes, the same," said Bright as the horseman moved forward and reined in facing the side of the wagon where she sat.

"Charles Cameron don't own slaves," the voice said.

Bright drew in her breath as she looked directly into

Toby's brown eyes. Her heart stopped as she looked at the gray hat shading a part of his face. He was even more handsome than she remembered.

He knows Papa does not believe in slavery, she thought. *He knows we have no slaves.* Her fear sent rivulets of cold sweat down her back and caused her fingertips to grow numb with cold. What could she do?

She met his steady gaze, his face unmoving as stone, while saying a silent prayer that he would not give her away, a prayer that would never make it to her lips.

"Toby," she whispered under her breath. She knew he could see her lips as he continued to look at her. She sat, unmoving except for her trembling hands hidden in the folds of the cloak.

Then, as if he were a wall she could lean against in her fear, Bright began to be aware that Marcus was breathing in rhythm with her, supporting her, although they sat some distance apart on the seat of the wagon. The slow breathing calmed her. Her fear grew less. *Thank you, Marcus*, she thought. *Thank you.*

Finally Toby spoke again, his voice shaking slightly. "Charles Cameron on top of the mountain out there? I've heard of him. He don't own slaves."

The horses stepped restlessly, rattling the harness. The night birds sang. The river roared. But no one spoke until Bright's heart joined the night noises resounding in her ears, sounding louder than any of them.

Finally, after what seemed an eternity to Bright, Toby spoke again.

"Your pa's that *other* Charles Cameron, the friend of Edward Haverford the slave owner in the low country, ain't he?" His voice seemed to be willing Bright to agree with him.

She nodded her head. "Yes," she said, almost breath-lessly.

"And he's a smithy, too, ain't he?" asked Toby, speaking slowly, deliberately.

"Yes," said Bright.

"I know him well. He used to boast to Mr. Haverford about his big buck Marcus all the time. I recognize these two. They are what they say they are," said Toby, his words coming in a rush as if he had found a solution to a problem and did not want to lose it.

"Then you will vouch for this pair?" said the first soldier.

Looking at Bright, his eyes growing more intense even in the shadow of the hat, Toby said quietly but firmly, "On my life."

"It still troubles me to leave a white woman out here with *him*," the first soldier said, nodding toward Marcus. "We ought to search them to be sure."

"That will not be necessary," said Toby, taking command of the situation. He continued to look intently at Bright. "This man will not harm a hair on this woman's head," Bright heard Toby say firmly as he moved his horse closer to Marcus, so that he was looking directly into the older man's eyes, as if warning him. "If he did, he knows what would happen to him. Don't you, *Marcus*?"

"Yes, sir," answered Marcus. Bright could see his eyes narrowing in the shadows as he looked directly at Toby, seeming to answer Toby's warning in kind. "I would defend this little lady with my life. She be as safe right here with me as with her own papa. I owes her papa my life, several times over. She be some safe with me."

Toby continued to look at Marcus, who met his gaze

calmly. Finally Toby seemed satisfied that all was well. He turned his horse and lifted his hat to Bright.

"Until the war is over," he said, holding her with his eyes.

"Until the war is over," she repeated, whispering, not quite sure what he meant. Or, for that matter, what she meant, either.

The soldiers followed Toby and galloped away. As they rounded the bend in the road, Bright heard shrieks of raucous laughter.

Marcus urged the team into a slow trot, moving away from Toby and the men as fast as they dared. The wagon motion comforted Bright for a few moments, then suddenly she began to sob. Turning toward Marcus, she hid her face in his shoulder and wept. He took the reins in one hand and patted her head with the other, just like Papa always did when she cried.

"There, there, Brightie," he said. "Everything is all right. We are safe now. You did a good job. I am right proud of you. Charles will be, too."

But she continued to sob. She could not control herself. She wasn't sure if she might be crying from relief or from joy at seeing Toby again.

"Miss Brightie, broken hearts do mend," he said softly. "But it takes time. And the young man, he told you that you have until the end of the war." Marcus laughed. "I wasn't born yesterday, little missy." He shook his head, chuckling at his memories.

"Do you think that is what he meant?" Bright finally asked Marcus.

"Brightie, what I think doesn't matter," said Marcus. "What you think and what that young man thinks, that's what matters. But he said, 'until the war is over.' In any case, he is the reason we are alive. Me, anyhow. That young man, he knows right from wrong. Why don't you take the reins for now?" Bright smiled to herself in the darkness. Mayhap she *would* see Toby again when the war was over.

Then she remembered the purpose of their journey and began to worry about the women and children hidden under the wagon floor. She turned around to knock three times. Her thumps were echoed softly by the women hiding there. They were all right.

"Do you think we'll get there safely?" Bright asked Marcus after a long silence.

"We are doing fine," he answered. "We meet more friends of yours, I know we'll be safe," he teased. "The four in the woods are all right, too."

"How do you know?" she asked.

Marcus made the sound of a mourning dove, low in his throat. His call was answered by four other mourning doves, three on one side of the road, and one on the other. Bright laughed in relief. No wonder she had been surprised that the mourning dove sounds were part of the night out here beside the river.

Silently they rode. The arc of the moon's journey overhead marked the hours. Bright held the reins and looked straight ahead as the eastern sky turned silver and pink with dawn. Her arms were almost numb, but Marcus seemed to sleep on the bench beside her. She hoped they could make it to the English farm before good daylight.

Hoofbeats sounded. "Want me to take the reins?" Marcus whispered, without seeming to move as six men in uniforms rode up behind them.

"No," she whispered.

CHAPTER 25 ⁊⊙

HER HANDS TREMBLING, Bright looked straight ahead while six horsemen rode single file past the wagon. With all the courage she could find in her fifteen-year-old self, she silently drew on the strength of Marcus, who seemed to sleep on the seat beside her, carefully matching her breathing to the slow rise and fall of his chest. Grateful for the calm she had seen Marcus display more than once, she marveled that the greater the danger and chaos around them, the more centered and quiet the tall man became. To an observer, his body appeared to be totally relaxed, but Bright knew that he was like a cat, poised and ready to spring.

Watching him breathe from the corner of her eye helped her to focus and quell her terror at the danger surrounding them—danger to the silent eyes hidden in the forest on either side, danger to herself, to Marcus, and to the others in her care. Breathing in tandem with Marcus, silently she prayed for their safety, for courage to meet the responsibilities that rested with her this night, and then she prayed that the horses would not tire before they reached the English farm upriver.

"Do you want me to take the reins?" Marcus whispered again, seeming to be inert, asleep, his lips almost still. From behind, the uniforms, more black than blue in the moonlight, passed single file and formed a cluster a few yards in front of them.

"No," answered Bright quietly. "I am in charge."

Marcus made no answer, but Bright sensed his acknowledgment.

The last of the uniformed men turned his horse abruptly around, causing Bright's team to rear. Struggling to control the horses and to keep the wagon upright, she was grateful as Marcus moved quickly forward to reach out and pull the reins, helping her to gain control.

"Where you headed, my pretty lady?" asked the soldier, sneering. "With a Negro in your wagon in the middle of the night? Be he slave? Or be he free?"

"Marcus belongs to my father," she said, working to keep her voice soft and steady. "We are delivering a load of rocks to stem a flood. Marcus has the responsibility of making sure I return to my father's farm safely. Here are his papers."

The man looked at the papers, shrugged, and handed them to his comrade. Bright realized that neither of the men could read, and she was much relieved.

"The papers look to be in order," said the first man, handing them back to Bright.

"We be looking for three Union deserters," said the other man. "Run from the Hungry River Union camp last week. You two sure don't fit that description. We ain't had no orders about slaves on the run. You wouldn't be a runaway slave, now would you?"

"Wouldn't no fool drive around with a runaway in her wagon in the middle of the night, anyways," said another man.

"If you see any uniforms or any brown faces around here," said the leader of the men, tipping his hat in Bright's direction, "you just send up a shot. We'll come a-running up here to help you, little lady, all the way from Pennsylvany, if need be." He spat a stream of tobacco juice into the underbrush growing on the embankment.

"Any brown faces or white faces, uniforms, anything, any day," said the other. "We'll come running."

"Thank you, gentlemen. I'll be sure to let you know," said Bright with a slight nod of her head, trying to keep the sarcasm out of her voice as she moved to cover her shaking hands with her cape. "*If* I need help."

Snapping the reins to urge the team back into the road as the horsemen broke into a gallop and rode on ahead of the wagon, Bright finally drew a deep breath and dared to look at the man beside her. He smiled and nodded in approval of her actions. She sighed in relief.

"Seen any Union soldiers? Deserters? Any brown faces?" asked Marcus quietly, still unmoving, but mocking the men with his voice, his face still, looking straight ahead. His eyebrows raised, his eyes dancing bright with moonlight as he looked away into a clearing lifted Bright's spirits. If Marcus could make light of the situation, then the danger must, at least for the moment, be past. Her father always said that Marcus had a gift for calming, and he did it most often by making light of the darkest situations.

To a watcher, she thought, Marcus would appear to simply be out for a drive, not facing threats to their lives and to the lives in their care. His pretense that all was normal comforted her, although she could not say just why it did so.

"Haven't seen many uniforms, but I have seen so many brown faces," said Bright, with a slight smile. "I wonder how many brown faces I *have* seen, both slave and free."

"You and me, both," said Marcus, shaking his head in wonderment and pride. "A long line, we have both seen, no doubt."

Even without closing her eyes, she could see a long line of brown faces, those who had been part of her life over the past nine years. And she knew how that long line of faces had changed her.

Bright smiled and looked around at the face of the man she had first seen when she had been a child. Marcus smiled back, and she saw the warm smile she had come to know and to love, the smile of her dear father's friend— a man who was a friend to so many who had passed through her father's smithy on their way to freedom.

Smiling and tugging at the reins, she pulled the team away from a rut in the embankment and whispered, "Yes, a long line of faces, all those who travel this path, a road that no one can see—an Underground Railroad, as Mr. Coffin says—the long road to freedom."

"A railroad that no one can see, that has no rails and no engines," whispered Marcus, taking the reins from her. "Slaves disappear, and no one sees them until they can sing bright freedom's song. Your papa named you well, Brightie."

"Tonight we travel that road together, Marcus," Bright said, taking her old friend's hand in hers, touching the scar with her fingers. "To carry on my papa's work.

And yours. And mine." Softly Marcus began to sing the song Papa had sung that summer day when they were riding in Caesar's carriage with the velvet cushions.

"I will sing again of a place called home," sang Marcus softly. Bright joined her soprano voice against his deep bass.

> "*A place where bright freedom's song can ring with the bells and sing through the skies,*
> *a place of bright freedom, a place of all glory, a place of bright freedom's song.*"

When they had finished singing, the rhythm of the song continued inside Bright's head. She had waited so long for this opportunity to do what she thought was the important work of her family. Even though she was fearful of the great responsibility for Marcus and the hidden slaves in her care, her feeling of exhilaration that the journey was almost ended made her heart sing, too.

"I have waited so long to be a part of this," she whispered to Marcus as he moved his head closer to hear her words. "To do this important work."

"But, Brightie, you have always been a part of the work, ever since that day you found me hiding in the henhouse," said Marcus softly. "Keeping secrets, peeling potatoes, keeping the hiding places clean, all these things are important, none more so than the others. We must all work together until all people on earth can sing bright freedom's song. You have been a part of this work since you were a little one," he reminded her.

Bright thought about his words. *Yes*, she thought, *even the smallest tasks play an important part in helping others to be free. And that makes me feel ever so good about my part in it.*

AFTERWORD ∂⌀

BRIGHT FREEDOM CAMERON did not exist, but she and her family might well have been residents of the Blue Ridge Mountains, the eastern range of the Appalachians near the borders of North Carolina, South Carolina, and Georgia. Families like hers might have been a part of the stories long neglected by history texts, stories of those who knew the horrors of bondage or whose parents knew the weight of chains and the pain of brands. The numbers of Americans who experienced that bondage, and who, I believe, risked everything to give aid to others who sought to escape, are greater than we know.

"We are, in fact, as Americans, the descendants of bound people . . . ," historian John Van der Zee wrote in *Bound Over: Indentured Servitude and American Conscience* (1985). Yet this facet of our history, which, according to some historians, has had a profound effect on the formative events and the basic tenets of our democracy, is largely ignored by general history texts.

Bound people included slaves and indentured servants, all those who lost their freedom and served in bondage, whatever the reason. Indentureship was first introduced into the American colonies because the new country needed residents and workers. The practice had long been common in the British Isles. There a person usually was indentured to repay a debt.

Experiences in indentured servitude influenced the history of our country in many ways. The roots of the Revolutionary War and the formation of the nation are believed to have grown out of the experiences of indentureship. The Abolitionist Movement had its roots in the experiences of New Englanders in indentureship. I believe that experiences in indentured servitude also influenced the activities of the yeoman farmers of the southern Appalachian Mountains, activities that enabled escaping slaves to reach freedom.

With their southern parameters in Georgia and Alabama and their northern tips in New England and Canada, the ranges of the Greater Appalachians run through almost every state in which slavery was legal. Therefore, they provided a protected route from the slave to the free states. Routes more easily traveled were available, yet most slaves walking overland took the difficult route through the coves and along the peaks of the Appalachians, a sparsely settled region with numerous natural caves and other hiding places. The oral storytelling tradition of the region tells of many Appalachian farmers who gave aid to escaping slaves and who actively opposed slavery.

When colonization of America began, the bondage of indentureship was used as a means for poor settlers to pay passage to cross the Atlantic. British noblemen and landlords also sold those they considered **undesirable** into indentureships to rid themselves and their neighboring counties of those they considered unfit to be their neighbors. Some peasants were sold to make room for sheep or hunting lands.

The original definition for *kidnap*, according to *Webster's Third International Dictionary*, was "to carry off (a person) to enforced labor in the British colonies in America. . . ." Many of the kidnapped were children and young adults from poor families who were already weak and malnourished.

In some places, four-fifths of indentured servants died during the first year, usually from cruel treatment such as whipping and branding for identification, starvation, lack of clothing and shelter, and illnesses, often caused by filth and lack of clean water and good food. Overall, one-third of indentured servants died before regaining their freedom.

For the voyage across the Atlantic, those in bondage were crowded into a stifling hold of the ship with insufficient food and water, and unsanitary conditions. "Putrid fever" claimed the lives of the weaker ones. Upon arrival, indentured servants were put through a "curing" period of one year, during which they were were given the poorest food and clothing, exposed to harsh weather, and given the most difficult jobs. Curing was used to eliminate those who would not live out their period of servitude.

Numerous documents and scholarly books indicate that once they had arrived in America, European indentured servants shared a status that was essentially the same as that of African slaves, except that the indentured had the legal status of persons, whereas slaves did not. Indentured servants would one day be granted full rights of free men and women. Slaves, who were bound for life, would never have such rights. Yet since few indentured servants had any knowledge of their legal rights, unscrupulous masters could mistreat and cheat them; and in practice, such rights were of little consequence.

For the period of indentureship, which could legally last from four to ten years, the indentured could be bought, sold, separated from family, abused, whipped, kept in chains or manacles, and branded, usually on the face, with a hot branding iron for identification. Their treatment did not differ from that of slaves, and in some cases, it was worse. Indentured servants, whose passage had cost the master only a small sum and who would leave when their service was over, legally could be hanged for running away, a punishment considered too wasteful for slaves because slaves involved a capital investment and a lifetime of service. When indentured servants escaped and were recaptured, their periods of servitude were usually extended by as much as a year for each day they were gone from the master's service, in some cases making the period of bondage lifelong.

At the end of servitude, colonial laws provided the newly freed indentured servant with one hundred acres of land, a small sum of money, and a new suit of clothes. Documented evidence suggests that some early leaders of the new country established their fortunes by illegally obtaining the land grants of indentured servants, who did not know they were to receive the land. This left the newly freed with no resources and with no choice but to walk to regions where land could be homesteaded, such as the valleys and ridges of the Appalachian Mountains.

Indentured servants emigrating from Europe were divided into three classes from the earliest days of the practice. The middle class included the largest number of indentured servants. Many of the early bonded servants of this class came from the poorer classes of England and from Scotland, Ireland, and Wales, who were often evicted from the small farms to which their families had been attached for generations. Many of this class were kidnapped—children and young people were regularly stolen and sold. The experiences of members of this middle class of servants are the experiences of Charles (Tearlach) Cameron.

The exportation of indentured servants was slowed by British laws enacted in the early 1800s to slow the emigration of the highest class of indentured servant, the trained artisans and craftspeople. The need for farm labor in America could not be filled with indentured servants. Northern Europeans accustomed to wearing dark woolen clothing did not survive for long on the large plantations of the South. Within a few years, the need for workers who could withstand the heat and humidity of large cotton and rice farms in southern coastal areas was filled by the expanding trade in African slaves.

After the American Revolution, German and Irish tradespeople and artisans made up a majority of indentured servants entering the United States legally, although the practice of illegal indentureship of the poor persisted. According to David Galenson (1981), the system existed into the twentieth century. The most recent immigrants to experience indentureship were the half million Asians who continued to arrive in bondage until several humanitarian groups succeeded in outlawing servitude in all forms in the United States in 1918.

I believe it is time that this part of our history, well-known to academic historians, became a part of our general knowledge.

BIBLIOGRAPHY ✑

Arthur, J. P. *Western North Carolina: A History from 1730 to 1913.* Johnson City, Tenn.: Overmountain Press, 1996. First published in 1914.

**Bailyn, B. *Voyagers to the West: A Passage in the Peopling of America on the Eve of the Revolution.* New York: Knopf, 1986.

**Blackmun, O. *Western North Carolina: Its Mountains and Its People to 1880.* Boone, N.C.: Appalachian Consortium Press, 1977.

**Breyfogle, W. A. *Make Free: The Story of the Underground Railroad.* Philadelphia, Pa.: Lippincott, 1958.

Coffin, L. "Reminiscences of Levi Coffin." In *The American Negro: His History and Literature.* Edited by W. L. Katz. New York: Arno Press and *New York Times.* First published in 1876, a copy is extant in the Moorland-Spinarn Collection, Howard University.

Dillon, M. L. *Slavery Attacked: Southern Slaves and their Allies, 1619–1865.* Baton Rouge, La.: Louisiana State Univ. Press, 1990.

Ellis, D. *Thrilling Adventures of Daniel Ellis, the Great Union Guide of East Tennessee for a Period of Nearly four years During the Great*

Southern Rebellion, Written by Himself. New York: Harper and Brothers, 1867; Johnson City, Tenn.: Overmountain Press, 1989.

Galenson, D. W. *White Servitude in Colonial America: An Economic Analysis.* Cambridge, England: Cambridge Univ. Press, 1981.

Graham, I. C. C. *Colonists from Scotland: Emigration to North America, 1707–1783.* Ithaca, N.Y.: American Historical Association, 1956.

Harrold, S. *The Abolitionists and the South, 1831–1861.* Lexington, Ky.: Univ. of Kentucky Press, 1995.

Jacobs, H. A. *Incidents in the Life of a Slave Girl Written by Herself.* Boston, Mass.: n.p., 1860. Edited by L. M. Child. Miami, Fla.: Mnemosyne Pub. Co., 1969.

Kennedy, B. *The Scots-Irish in the Carolinas.* Belfast, Northern Ireland: Ambassador Productions, Ltd., 1997.

Meyer, D. G. *The Highland Scots of North Carolina, 1732–1776.* Chapel Hill, N.C.: Univ. of North Carolina Press, 1961.

O'Neill, J. *So Far from Skye.* London: Puffin Books, 1992.

Rawick, G. P., ed. *The American Slave: A Composite Autobiography, North Carolina Narratives,* pts. 1 and 2, vols. 14 and 15. Westport, Conn.: Greenwood Pub. Co., 1941, 1972.

Smedley, R. C. "History of the Underground Railroad." In *The American Negro: His History and Literature.* Edited by W. L. Katz. New York: Arno Press and *New York Times,* 1969.

Smith, A. E. *Colonists in Bondage: White Servitude and Convict Labor in America 1607–1776.* Chapel Hill, N.C.: Univ. of North Carolina Press, 1965.

Snith, W. B. *White Servitude in Colonial South Carolina.* Columbia, S.C.: Univ. of South Carolina Press, 1961.

Stampp, K. M. *America in 1857: A Nation on the Brink.* Oxford, England: Oxford Univ. Press, 1990.

Still, W. "The Underground Railroad." In *The American Negro: His History and Literature.* Edited by W. L. Katz. New York: Arno Press and *New York Times,* 1968.

Taylor, R. H. "Slaveholding in North Carolina: An Economic View." In *The James Sprunt Historical Publications.* Edited by

R. D. W. Connor, et al. Chapel Hill, N.C.: Univ. of North Carolina Press, 1926.

Trotter, W. R. *Bushwhackers! The Mountains.* Winston-Salem, N.C.: J. F. Blair, 1988.

**Van der Zee, J. *Bound Over: Indentured Servitude and American Conscience.* New York: Simon and Schuster, 1985.

**especially helpful in writing this book

OTHER HELPFUL REFERENCES

Duke University, William R. Perkins Library, Broadside Collection, "Slave Voices" exhibits, documents from Special Collections. Provides words typically used to describe black Americans in documents of the period. web site: http://scriptorium.lib.duke.edu

U.S. Department of the Interior, "Underground Railroad" web sites: http://www.nps.gov/undergroundrr/contents.htm http://www.nps.gov/crweb1/history/ugrr.htm

MacGowan Clan web site; The Highland Clearances Information web site: http://www.sirius.com/~macgowan/hc.html